BENEATH THE SUN

BENEATH THE SUN

Claire Lorrimer

CHIVERS
THORNDIKE

This Large Print edition is published by BBC Audiobooks Ltd, Bath, England and by Thorndike Press, Waterville, Maine, USA.

Published in 2004 in the U.K. by arrangement with the Author.

Published in 2004 in the U.S. by arrangement with Claire Lorrimer

U.K. Hardcover   ISBN 0–7540–9910–5 (Chivers Large Print)
U.K. Softcover   ISBN 0–7540–9911–3 (Camden Large Print)
U.S. Softcover   ISBN 0–7862–6266–4 (General)

The text of this Large Print edition is unabridged.
Other aspects of the book may vary from the original edition.

Set in 16 pt. New Times Roman.

Printed in Great Britain on acid-free paper.

British Library Cataloguing in Publication Data available

Library of Congress Control Number: 2003115247

PROLOGUE 1987

'It's so unfair, Gran! I may never get another chance to go to Egypt. Lucy will find someone else to go on holiday with her—and it wouldn't have cost Mum and Dad a penny. It's so unfair . . .'

Mrs Barlow senior patted the girl's hair, and drew her down on the sofa beside her. This fourteen year old was her first and—secretly— her favourite grandchild. She looked so like her father, Chris!

'So Mum and Dad haven't told you why they don't want you to go!' she commented. 'But I'm going to do so. You see, my dear, something very frightening happened to them many years ago—long before you were born. They don't like to talk about it because it brings back so many unpleasant memories.'

The girl stared at her grandmother, wide-eyed with curiosity.

'Go on, Gran,' she urged.

'They were going on their honeymoon. It was 1969. Your father had booked rooms for them in a hotel in Cairo . . . but they never got there!'

Her grand-daughter nodded.

'Mum said they were diverted to Tripoli— that's in Libya, isn't it? But she never told me why they changed their plans—just that there

1

was a hitch in the arrangements. So what happened, Gran? And what can it possibly have to do with me going to Egypt with Lucy?'

Her grandmother smiled.

'If you sit still and stop fidgeting, I'll tell you!' she said, her smile fading as she added: 'It happened like this . . .'

1969

CHAPTER ONE

Mary-Lou put the last lunch tray in the rack and smoothed the dark hair from her forehead with a sigh.

'That's done that. Do you want a cup of coffee, Eve?'

The pretty blonde stewardess, Mary-Lou's senior by two years' service, smiled and nodded.

Because of the extreme smallness of the tiny galley it was necessary for both girls to confine their physical movement to the minimum. In the eighteen months of working together they had managed to achieve a perfect partnership, each knowing what was to be done and how to carry out their tasks with the minimum inconvenience to the other as they moved around the plane.

The big V.C.10 was very far from full today. Two coaches carrying passengers to the airport had failed to arrive on time and although they had delayed take-off to the last possible limit, the plane had had to leave finally with a complement of only thirty-four passengers. Consequently their job of serving lunch had been comparatively easy and they could relax for a while—or at least until one of the

3

passengers rang for attention.

Both girls had become very efficient at summing up the passengers and their potential for being 'a nuisance'. As they had taken their seats on boarding the plane at Heathrow, Mary-Lou reckoned this could well be an easy flight. Apart from the limited numbers, there were no babies or young children who usually inevitably meant more work for her and Eve, and the adults looked a reasonable group.

The couple in seats One and Two were obviously newly-weds, possibly on their honeymoon. They were too engrossed in each other to be much trouble to anyone! Across the aisle from them were a middle-aged couple, Mr and Mrs James, with their daughter. The girl, ash blonde and very thin, looked as if she might have been ill—probably going to a hot climate to recuperate, Mary-Lou decided. It amused her, when she had time, to try to guess the background of her passengers, though it could be a tantalizing pastime since she seldom knew by the end of the trip whether she had guessed right or wrong.

She had been right about the elderly couple in Eleven and Twelve, though. Harold and Elsie Curry, old-age pensioners, were on their first and probably their last trip abroad, for which they had been saving for years and years. The old girl had been a bit nervous when the plane took off and her husband,

4

devoted and caring, had confided the details to Mary-Lou when she stopped for a few minutes to reassure his wife. They had a married daughter in South Africa and were paying her a visit. They hadn't seen her for twenty years, and their three grandchildren never. Mrs Curry had calmed down once they were at cruising height and had been no more trouble, poor dear.

Eve Cunningham was thoughtfully stirring the hot coffee in her plastic cup.

'I rather fancy the American in Twenty-eight!' she said with a twinkle in her large grey-green eyes. 'I think he'd try to date me if he dared!'

'Which American?' Mary-Lou asked, amused. There were two halfway up the cabin, one in his mid-forties, the other ten years or so younger.

'The young one, of course!' Eve said. 'His name is Bruce Mallory—I looked him up on the passenger list.'

'The red-haired one?'

Eve nodded.

'I think he's some kind of p.a. to the other, Kennedy Maxwell. *He's* in the Diplomatic. They're getting off at Cairo.'

Mary-Lou laughed.

'You seem to know a lot about them. Remember the rules, Eve—no chatting up the passengers!'

Eve sighed.

5

'That's one of the snags in this job—you see someone you could really go for and they alight next stop and you never see them again! Ah, well, such is life!'

Mary-Lou had no such problems. She was engaged—unofficially—to the second pilot, John Wilson. Married stewardesses were frowned on by the company so she and John couldn't take the plunge yet, but both were quite sure they wanted marriage eventually. For the time being Mary-Lou, who was only twenty-two and loved her job, was in no hurry to settle down, though John, six years her senior, was apt to be a bit jealous and possessive. He wanted marriage because it would tie Mary-Lou securely to him. But he'd agreed to wait until she was ready to make the final commitment.

The light flashed above Eve's head.

'I'll go,' she said as Mary-Lou stood up. It was one of the nice things about Eve— although she was senior, she always took her full share of the jobs.

She came back a moment later, her eyes full of laughter.

'It was that deb in number Six. Wants a brandy. And guess what, Mary-Lou—the blond-haired Liverpudlian sitting next to her is her boy-friend.'

'Are you sure?' Mary-Lou asked. 'They came on board acting as if they were strangers. Let's have a look at the passenger list. I'm sure

I know his face. It's my guess he's a pop singer—well known, too.'

The young girl was travelling under the name of Susan Smith—'An alias if ever there was one!' Eve said. The boy's name was listed as Henry Bard.

Suddenly, Mary-Lou gasped and clutched Eve's arm.

'I know who he really is!' she cried. 'He's Larry Bell and he *is* a pop singer—belongs to that band, First Impressions.'

'Never heard of them!' Eve grimaced. 'Don't tell me you're a fan, Mary-Lou!'

The younger girl grinned.

'No, but you haven't heard the rest of it!' she said excitedly. 'That girl he's with—she's no more Susan Smith than I am. She's the Honourable Sarah Finnon-Waters and in today's *Express* it said her parents had made her a ward of court because they believed she was eloping to Gretna Green with Larry Bell. Don't you see, Eve, they've slipped the net somehow and next thing they'll be safely out of the court's jurisdiction and getting married in South Africa!'

Eve drew a deep breath.

'If you're right, we'd better tell Bob,' she said, referring to the first pilot. 'He'll know what to do.'

'Radio the news back home, I suppose,' Mary-Lou said doubtfully. 'Maybe we shouldn't say anything, Eve. After all, *I could* be wrong.'

Eve raised her eyebrows.

'But you don't think so. Anyway, we ought to consider the girl. She doesn't look a day over sixteen to me. And if she is the Hon. someone or other, it's understandable her parents want to stop her marrying a chap like that.'

'She's sixteen!' Mary-Lou agreed, quelling her romantic instincts. 'Not really old enough to know her own mind.'

Eve did not hesitate further. Bob Sinclair was a mature married man of forty-five. He had a daughter in her teens. Let him decide what to do. She got up and went through the cabin towards the cockpit. Passing between the rows of passengers, she glanced at them automatically, wearing the pleasant relaxed smile she could assume at will. Most of the passengers smiled back. The group of dark-skinned athletes grinned cheerfully. They were members of a football team from somewhere in Africa who'd been in England playing a series of friendly matches.

But three African gentlemen up front did not smile. Eve grimaced to herself. She held no racial prejudices but she didn't like the look of the scowling dark faces. There was something almost furtive about all three of them.

Their scowls were compensated by the friendly smile of the young red-haired American she'd remarked upon to Mary-Lou.

8

His companion was engrossed in an official-looking document and Eve paused briefly.

'Anything you'd like, sir?' she asked professionally.

Bruce Mallory's smile widened. His eyes twinkled mischievously. Despite herself, Eve felt the colour come into her cheeks.

'I'm just fine, thank you, ma'am!' he said.

She moved on hurriedly, chiding herself for letting anyone embarrass her. At twenty-six, she was long past the age of blushing when attractive young men propositioned or flirted with her. In her job it was practically an everyday occurrence and she had become adept over the years at coldly rebuffing the advances made. The difference now, she knew very well, was that she didn't particularly wish to rebuff Mr Bruce Mallory. She liked his bronzed lean face and wide smiling mouth. She liked the deep-set hazel eyes, full of laughter yet with an underlying intelligence beneath. She wished very much that he wasn't a passenger and that she'd met him in other circumstances where she could have got to know him better.

It was two years now since she'd ended an unhappy affair with one of the other pilots. It had been a crazy, unsatisfactory, stupid affair since she'd known from the beginning that he was married and merely amusing himself. But she'd fallen in love for the first time in her life and had been in too deep too quickly to avoid the inevitable pitfalls that attended such a relationship. Finally, she'd found the courage to make the break and was beginning at last to recover the pieces of her broken heart; even occasionally to wonder if it had been quite so severely broken as she had imagined at the time. Now, with a deep inner awareness of release, she realised that she was actually capable of being attracted by another man; a completely different man from her first lover. Tall, thin, angular, red-headed, Bruce Mallory bore not the slightest resemblance to the square, fair-haired one-time rugby player who'd seduced her with such ease!

Conscious of the young American's eyes on her back, she went through to the cockpit and closed the door between them. But she knew it would be only a matter of minutes before she had to face him again and was certain that he would be watching for her. She felt excited and self-conscious—young again, and even more regretful that in a few hours' time, he would be disembarking at Cairo Airport and that she'd probably never see him again.

John Wilson, second pilot, yawned, stretched and stood up as Eve came into the cockpit. He was a pleasant-looking, rather ordinary young man but his smile had great charm and Eve could understand why Mary-Lou found him both attractive and, as a character, likeable. He was good-tempered, amusing, friendly, and he worshipped

Mary-Lou.

He said now:

'Since you're here, Eve, I'll nip along and have a word with Mary-Lou. Okay, Skipper?'

Bob Sinclair nodded. He knew all the ins and outs of his co-pilot's romance with the young stewardess and in his kind, good-natured way, helped John whenever and however he could. He knew how passionately anxious John was to tie Mary-Lou down and understood why. There was always a danger of a girl as pretty as that meeting someone else.

When John had left, Eve told Bob and Jimmy Tate, the radio operator, about the young couple, adding that she and Mary-Lou thought they could be elopers.

'I don't know if it's any of our business or if we should keep our suspicions to ourselves,' she ended. 'Mary-Lou is pretty sure the boy is Larry Bell though, and the girl is certainly young and well spoken. What do you think? They're going as far as South Africa.'

Bob Sinclair sighed. He was thinking of his own pop-crazy daughter when he said:

'If the kid's only sixteen, then we ought to radio back.' He glanced at his watch. 'We land at Cairo in a couple of hours—doesn't leave them much time to organise someone to be there to meet them.' He hoped they wouldn't be held up on landing as a result. At forty-five he was beginning to feel tired at the end of these long trips and realised that when the

11

time came in the near future for him to retire, he wouldn't be sorry. He was still very much in love with his wife, Lilian, and he looked forward to a more settled routine life in their pleasant country cottage at Chertsey. His son and daughter were growing up fast and it wouldn't be long before they left home. He'd have Lilian to himself and . . .

'Do not make any false move, Captain. I have a gun at your back!'

Just for a split second of time, Bob Sinclair thought the man's voice behind him was that of John, playing some silly schoolboy prank. But as he slowly turned his head, he glimpsed the white startled faces of Eve and Jimmy and then the dark African features of the speaker.

To his intense surprise the man did have a gun pointing at him. Bob blinked stupidly, trying to take in the improbability of the situation. The question flashed through his mind whether the man was drunk or mad or both. He was aware of danger and felt his muscles tense.

The man's mouth tightened.

'If you disobey me, I shall not hesitate to shoot!' he said, in a heavily accented voice.

'Don't be stupid!' Bob said sharply, and bluffing, added: 'We're at thirty thousand feet. If a bullet went through the fuselage, the air pressure would blow us all to hell.'

There was a flicker of surprise on the man's face.

'Do not take me for a fool. I know a bullet would have no such effect. I have two colleagues back there. Each has a machine-gun. We could kill many people if you force us. Please make up your mind now to obey me.'

For the first time, Eve spoke. Frightened though she was, she could not yet bring herself to believe in the reality of this scenario. Any moment now, John Wilson would return. With luck he'd take the man by surprise.

'What is it you want?' she asked as coolly as if she were enquiring of one of her passengers what they would like to drink.

'You will alter course!' the man replied, equally imperturbably. 'You will fly to Northern Nigeria. There you will be signalled where to land.'

'Are you crazy?' Bob burst out tactlessly. 'This is a commericial aeroplane. I have nearly forty people on board. We're due to land at Cairo in a couple of hours. I can . . .'

'You will do as I say. Believe me, Captain, I *mean* what I say. My men have machine-guns. Neither you nor any of your passengers will live if you disobey. Please alter course now.'

Instinctively both Bob's and Jimmy Tate's hands moved towards the radio controls but neither was quick enough. The man hit both the pilot and the radio operator sharp blows across the sides of their heads with the gun butt. Blood poured from the cut on Bob's temple and Eve cried out. She, in turn,

13

received a cuff sufficiently painful to silence her. With clear cut intent, their assailant now smashed the radio controls.

'Better do as he says!' Jimmy muttered.

'That is wise! I'm sure, Captain, you cannot be unfamiliar with the successes that have been had in the past when others like us have hi-jacked planes? A little co-operation from you will make everything very much pleasanter for everyone.'

'What's the idea behind it?' Bob asked. 'Why Nigeria? What's your objective?'

For a moment, the white teeth gleamed in the black face.

'I am Sabuco Engarri, leader of the revolutionary force who will overthrow the government. My army is in hiding and waits only my arrival to start marching. Since we cannot enter our country legally, we have no other alternative but to commandeer your plane . . .'

He broke off, as if suddenly aware that he might be revealing too much.

'The passengers are going to start asking questions soon,' Eve murmured. 'You'll never get away with it.'

'You are wrong. It will be in your hands to calm the passengers. Any trouble from them and I shall not hesitate to end your life, or that of the other young lady.'

'Better go along with him,' Bob said, and in an undertone, '. . . for the time being.' He

14

raised his voice again. 'Go and tell the passengers we've had to alter course because of freak weather conditions. Say we won't be landing at Cairo at the estimated time, not to worry and that you'll serve tea meanwhile. That should keep them quiet for a bit. And send John back here.'

Eve was permitted to leave the cockpit. Her mind was working furiously. She would, of course, tell John what was going on, but even if he were able to overpower the man in the cockpit she couldn't see how he could tackle the other two troublemakers in the cabin. It was too risky. For all she knew, they might use those wretched machine-guns—if they did in fact have them.

As she passed Bruce Mallory he smiled. But this time she could not return the smile. She wondered what he would do if he knew what was happening. Somehow she must put him in the picture. He was young and strong. He'd be able to help if there were trouble.

She glanced at the other passengers with a new look. Now she was not concerned with their physical comforts—merely to gauge which of the men could be counted on in an emergency. The coloured football team who occupied the middle block of seats on both sides of the aisle? She doubted it. If this was a racial issue, they might well side with the hijackers. Derby and Joan? No, too old. The three girls in their twenties opposite them?

They might or might not panic. The pop singer? Doubtful. Likewise the very smart woman with the grey-haired companion who looked as if she might be a nannie. The honeymoon husband might be an asset. But the couple with the daughter did not look as if they could offer much help. The girl looked ill and both her parents were engrossed in her. In other circumstances Eve would have stopped to enquire if the girl needed anything.

Blissfully ignorant of the disaster that had descended upon them, John Wilson and Mary-Lou were quietly embracing.

'Break it up!' Eve said sharply as she entered the galley. 'Trouble with a capital T!'

As briefly and succinctly as possible she put them in the picture.

'Radios are u.s.!' she said. 'It's us against three men, one with a revolver and two with machine-guns. Bob's had to fly south.'

For a moment they thought she was joking. But a closer look at Eve's white taut face assured them she was not. They took it surprisingly well.

'I'm going to put out a soothing message on the tannoy,' Eve went on. 'You'd better go back, John, but be careful. The man has already hit Bob and Jimmy, not to mention yours truly. Mary-Lou, you start on teas. It'll give them something else to think about. Whatever we do, we don't want a panic. I'm going to dispense free drinks to the Americans

16

and the newly-weds, together with a slip of paper looking like a bill but telling them what's up. Okay?'

John hesitated, obviously unwilling to go back up front.

'I don't like to leave you two girls alone!' he said doubtfully.

'Nonsense, sweetie!' Mary-Lou told him. 'We'll be okay. Besides, you can't leave Bob and Jimmy coping on their own. Don't worry, darling. Eve and I will survive. No one's going to hurt us.'

He left them, though obviously still very worried.

Quickly Eve scribbled two notes, on one side of which she put the cost of the drink, on the other the somewhat dramatic statement: *We've been hi-jacked. Three Africans, front seats, have guns. Pilot made to alter course for Nigeria.* She put two brandies on two drink trays, placed the bill slips under the glasses and carried them back into the cabin.

The newly-wed, Chris Barlow, looked up in surprise as she put the drink in front of him. From the corner of her eye Eve could see one of the Africans leaning over the arm of his seat watching her down the aisle.

'Compliments of the airline, sir!' she said in a loud bright voice, and pushed the bill towards Barlow. As he picked it up, still looking puzzled, Eve saw that he had noticed the writing. With a sigh of relief she moved on

17

up the aisle.

She realised that this next delivery was not going to be quite so simple. The two Africans were seated directly in the row in front of the Americans. Anything said was bound to be over-heard by them.

She gave Bruce Mallory a forced smile. 'Here's your brandy, sir. Sorry I've been so long!'

She saw his eyebrows shoot up and kicked him swiftly on the leg. She felt an hysterical desire to giggle. He must think she was trying to pick him up! His companion was staring at her over the top of his horn-rimmed glasses. Before either could speak, she chattered on quickly: 'That'll be three and six, sir. Would you mind paying now?'

Bruce Mallory shrugged. He hadn't ordered a brandy, didn't want one and couldn't make out why the stewardess had brought it. Least of all did he understand why the girl had just kicked him. He was quite sure he'd not been mistaken. That kick had been clear and deliberate.

He picked up the slip of pink paper. She said:

'The cost of the drink is on the other side, sir!'

Now Bruce felt he was beginning to understand. The girl was trying to give him a message in secret. He was amused—and a bit surprised. He'd liked the look of her—thought

18

her more than a little attractive; though not the type who'd take to being propositioned. In a way he'd been glad. He didn't admire women who were too easy. He'd set this one above that class and was a little disappointed to find her trying to pick him up.

He was embarrassed, too, knowing his boss, Kennedy Maxwell, was quizzing him and trying to read the note over the top of his glasses. The girl was still waiting. For the money? For an answer?

He read the note and glanced up quickly, his manner instantly alert and wary. Eve's grey-green eyes met his steadily. She lowered her lids just once, deliberately, as if answering his unspoken question. So it was serious! He slipped the note across to Maxwell. He'd better be in the know too. A few minutes ago, when the girl's educated English voice had tannoyed the change of course and spoken of freak weather conditions, Maxwell had commented on the message.

'Weather looks okay to me!' he had said in that deep but rather staccato voice of his. 'Wonder what's up?'

A clever, efficient diplomat, Kennedy Maxwell was sparing with his words, seldom speaking unless he had something worth saying and then saying exactly what he meant. Bruce, who'd been his personal assistant for four years, greatly admired the man, respected his ability as highly as he did the strong integral character that went with it. A year ago, Bruce had been offered an up-grading to a more senior post in Washington but had opted to remain as Maxwell's p.a. Money and position weren't everything, he'd told himself at the time. As Maxwell's p.a. he travelled the world, saw life with a capital L and learned far, far more than ever he would at a desk in Washington.

He'd not regretted the decision and he knew, though Maxwell had only mentioned it once, that his boss was grateful for his loyalty as much as for the hard behind-the-scenes work he put in regardless of self interest.

He gave the stewardess the correct change and asked her to bring another brandy for Mr Maxwell. It would give them time to consider the fantastic position they were apparently now in—write a message back to her. Poor kid! She must be scared out of her wits, though she didn't look it!

Kennedy Maxwell screwed the pink paper into a tiny ball. He picked up his gold fountain pen and began writing on the front of the document he was holding. Bruce read over his shoulder:

Get my hand luggage down from the rack. There is a small gun in one of the two electric shaving kits. Might come in handy. Give this to the girl when she brings my drink.

And he handed Bruce a dollar bill on which he wrote in minute letters the cryptic message:

Have gun. Any use?

Eve returned almost at once with the second brandy. Bruce gave her the dollar bill and saw her eyes look for and find the message. Deliberately he began a flirtation with her, his voice raised so that the two men in the front seat could not possibly fail to hear him. He wanted a feasible excuse for keeping in touch with Eve and this would seem as natural as any.

'You're a mighty pretty girl!' he drawled. 'How about a date when we land? They say there's quite a bit of night life in Cairo. How about it, honey?'

For a moment Eve looked taken aback. But his voice was so drawled, so exaggeratedly American, that she quickly realised he was talking for the sake of the eavesdroppers up front.

'Maybe!' she said. 'I'll think about it. Ask me again later. I'm busy right now. I've got to help the other stewardess do teas!'

'Sure, honey. You come right on back just as soon as you can. Say, sweetheart, do all you English girls have those gorgeous complexions and long long legs?'

Despite the gravity of the situation, Eve nearly laughed. 'I'm afraid I don't know, sir,' she answered demurely. 'I really must go now and see to the teas. I'll be back as soon as I can.'

She left with some reluctance. The

21

nonsense they had both been talking had been strangely reassuring. It was as if they had established a kind of code unrecognisable to the hi-jackers.

She was stopped on the way back to the galley by the couple with the daughter. They looked worried. 'Will it be a long delay?' the man asked anxiously. 'My daughter Jennifer—she's not very well. How late do you think we'll be?'

'I'm afraid I can't say just now, sir,' Eve answered with a quick professional look at the girl sitting between her parents. She did look ill. Her face was twitching and deathly white. Eve tried to concentrate on her nurse's training. What was wrong with the girl?

'Anything I can get for your daughter?' she asked.

The mother looked at her timorously. She seemed almost as nervous and ill at ease as her daughter.

'It's all right. Jennifer will be all right!' she said in a small high voice.

'We'll be bringing tea round in a minute,' Eve said. 'Perhaps a nice cup of tea would . . .'

'She's all right. It's just—well, please let us know as soon as you know how long overdue we'll be,' the father broke in. 'My daughter has been . . . ill. She's going into hospital as soon as we arrive. Naturally, I'm concerned. You understand?'

Eve caught the undertones of anxiety and

gave the girl another searching look. What *was* wrong? Not heart. Pregnant? No! Why didn't the father say what was the matter?

'I've had nursing training, sir,' she said. 'If there is anything I could get your daughter...?'

But both the man and woman shook their heads. The girl did not open her eyes. She seemed totally unaware of Eve's presence, or even of her own. Whatever she suffered, it engrossed her completely.

Eve was worried.

She mentioned it to Mary-Lou who by now had made two huge pots of tea and was preparing the trays with cups, saucers, paper packets of sugar and plastic spoons.

'Something wrong with the James girl in Number Four,' Eve cautioned. 'Keep an eye on her.'

Mary-Lou nodded.

'I noticed earlier. She was sleeping all through lunch. I reckoned they'd overdone the tranquillisers or air-sick pills or something. She looked drugged to me.'

Suddenly Eve understood. The girl wasn't ill in the ordinary sense of the word. She was a drug addict. If her guess was correct it explained the furtive way the parents were behaving, as if they were ashamed of the girl's illness—and frightened, too.

But she had no time to think further of the sick girl. It took a good quarter of an hour to

23

serve all the teas and the moment she could do so, she took a tray up to the cockpit. She needed desperately to know what was going on up there. For all she was aware, that horrible man with the gun could have shot Bob, John and Jimmy and taken over the controls!

It was almost a relief to find all three in their seats and the African standing where she had left him, at their backs, still holding the gun.

CHAPTER TWO

Leanora Carson lay back in her seat, eyes closed as if she were sleeping. She had heard the noise of the tea-trays being placed in front of her and Nanny but although she would not have objected to a cup of tea, she preferred to retain the impression that she was sleeping. That way, she could avoid talk.

She could picture quite clearly the grey-haired, neat, trim little figure in navy blue suit, sitting beside her, neat white shirt with clean, neat white collar and cuffs; sensible thick lisle stockings and neat, sensible brogue shoes. Clean and neat. Kind and neat. Trained, experienced, capable Edith Hurst—once a nanny, always a nanny. Leanora Carson had known within the first few minutes of the interview that she would engage her. The woman was everything she wanted, capable of taking all the responsibilites, unflappable, dependable . . .

'Oh God!' Leanora Carson shouted into the black isolation of her thoughts. 'Help me. I cannot bear it!'

Where was the God of her childhood? Where the kindly, all-loving, all-giving God of nursery days? God's will be done. And it *was* being done—with a vengeance; with the price of her life. No, not her life, her life's happiness . . . and Peter's. Don't forget Peter.

'Darling, where are you? *How* are you? Tell me.'

But of course he couldn't. She herself had extracted the promise. No letters. Never, ever, ever . . .

'I am thirty-two years old. I may live until I am eighty-two. For half a century, I shall have to live without Peter . . . without knowing . . .

'No!' she told herself sharply. Not to think like this. 'Don't think of now. Think of . . .'

But what to think of? Granville, her husband, waiting at the airport to meet her? How annoyed he'd be at the delay. Punctual to the second himself, he abominated unpunctuality. Well, it wouldn't be her fault. She didn't care if they never arrived . . .

Granville, Lt.-Col., Granville Waterman Carson would be planning as he planned everything in detail, the evening of her return home; The Return of the Prodigal Wife.

25

But no, he was mercifully ignorant of her prodigality. When she'd left him three months ago to go back to London for medical treatment, he had had not the very faintest idea that she was going to be unfaithful to him. Nor had she . . .

'Oh, Leanora, adding lies to your sins!' she told herself reproachfully, bitterly. 'You knew very well that when you saw Peter again, you'd be in bed with him within the hour! Peter! Peter! where are you? Are you thinking of me? Are you as desolate, as dead as I am? But I am not dead. I feel and it hurts, it hurts . . . Will it ever stop hurting? Will my whole life—all fifty years to come—be one long pain?

'I will not think of Peter. I will remember Granville, probably this very minute ordering his car and telling Ted, his driver, to be ready to set out for the airport.' How precisely Granville always made his wants known. He was never obtuse. There was no wondering what Granville meant when he spoke.

'Leanora, I shall sleep in your room tonight!'

No, no doubting Granville's intentions. Even their nights of sex were planned and announced ahead. Poor Granville; poor, simple, good, worthy, unimaginative man; first-class soldier, bottom-class lover. That wasn't fair. He did love her in his own terrible way. And it might not have been so terrible to a different kind of woman.

26

'Why did I do it? Why did I marry him?'

She knew the answer of course. Peter had become engaged to someone else.

'You should have *known* I'd never go through with it!' How reproachfully Peter had spoken. 'You should have *known* I loved you, Leanora. My only love. Always, my *only* love!'

But it wasn't true. He'd thought he loved that silly, empty-headed, fatuous, beautiful Sally. He'd loved Sally enough to ask her to marry him and Sally had said yes. How could she, Leanora, have known it would all be over before the year's end?

'You *should have waited!*'

'Ah, Peter, so easy to say now but how was I to know? And I hated you. I hated you so much for hurting me. I wanted to hurt you back. I married Granville to show you how little I cared.'

A long, deep sigh escaped from Leanora's closed lips. She sensed the glance her newly engaged nanny gave her and kept her eyes tightly closed. *She* had nothing to worry about. Granville would be the kind of man Nanny would approve of—no nonsense. And Paul, her five-year-old son, spitting image of his father in looks and character . . . yes, Nanny would approve of him, too.

Wistfully, Leanora wondered whether Paul would be excited at the prospect of seeing her this evening. He'd been staying with their friends, Julie and Bill Dekker, who had a small

27

boy her son's age. Paul seemed happier in their house than in his own! But she ought not to let this hurt her. It was natural that he should enjoy the company of another five-year-old. Besides, the boys could play soldiers all day long and it was Paul's passion in life to be a soldier—like Daddy.

'I am a wicked woman. I do not really love my son. I do not love my husband. I love only . . .'

'Peter, how can I bear it? You said I was the strong one of the two of us but I am weak, weak. If this plane landed at London Airport by mistake, I'd never be able to go through with it a second time; I'd never be able to leave you.

'If I could only sleep—forget for a little while! I could take one of my sleeping pills but then tonight, when I need it, I would be wide awake. Poor Granville. Tonight I cannot be a wife to you . . . no matter how carefully you have planned our reunion. Tonight I shall be dead with fatigue. I shall take two pills and sleep, sleep . . .'

Last night, they had had no sleep—the last night she would ever spend with Peter. How beautiful and how terrible those hours had been.

'Love-making and heart-breaking,' she thought. 'Words won't really describe the joy, the agony. I am paying for my sins. I am having my hell now, God. But I have had my glimpse

28

of heaven, too.'

But it had been so brief, so very brief. At first they had not talked much about the future. It was enough to be together, to be in love, to have the haven of Peter's flat where they could love one another world without end.

'My beautiful Leanora. Everything about you pleases and excites me; your long golden hair, your brown skin . . .'

But the rest was lost in kisses, desperate, hungry, impatient kisses; gentle, tender, satiated kisses; exploring kisses; exciting kisses. *'Kisses enough to circle the world, my beautiful Leanora!'*

'I shall never kiss him again. I will never know his kisses again. Had I known there must be an end to kissing, would I have asked for more? But no, there were always as many as I wanted.'

Within two weeks, they had known that she could not go back to Granville.

'You know what this means, Peter? I am a Roman Catholic. I can never marry you.'

'We are married already!'

'Ah, Peter, but in spirit only.'

She would have to live outside her Church. Shameful it might have been, but she did not care. She could live without anything or anyone but Peter.

'Would he give you the boy, Leanora?'

Her son, too, she would forfeit. Granville

would never let him go and she wouldn't take him. The child would at least be some compensation to him.

'You'll write and tell him—now? At once?'

But she hadn't done so. It could wait until tomorrow or the next day. She wasn't in a hurry to hurt Granville who couldn't help it that she didn't love him; that she loved Peter.

Then it happened. The first time, she had told herself that the change of climate, her nervous emotional state had been responsible for the missed date in the month. She had thought of a hundred and one reasons why—but never the real one.

'Liar!' she told herself. 'You know that isn't true. At least be honest with yourself since you couldn't be honest with Peter. You did wonder once or twice if you could be pregnant. But you didn't want to believe it. You didn't want to think about it. You hated the very idea of bearing Granville another child. You hid the suspicion of the truth even from yourself!'

But the second month she could no longer pretend. She went to the clinic and had a pregnancy test. It was irrefutably positive.

How long—how many days and nights before she could bring herself to tell Peter? How many excuses did she think up why she hadn't written to Granville about the divorce? How many hours of talk about the future, hers and Peter's, before she finally broke down and told him the truth.

'Oh, Peter, I didn't mean to hurt you. I couldn't help it.'

'But for God's sake, darling, surely you can get rid of it? You say you don't want it. It's legal now. Why not? For pity's sake, tell me why not?'

How to make him understand that for her, abortion must always be murder? A mortal sin—far, far worse than leaving Granville and living in sin with Peter. As a Catholic, she could not get rid of her child, Granville's child, a child of God no matter how much she might desire that it never be born.

Once, and only once, she had nearly weakened. Peter, desperate, had offered to accept the child as his own.

'At least it is half yours, my darling. I'd learn to love it if I had to. Better a thousand times than losing you. You can't go back to him, Leanora. I love you. I need you.'

But the priest had been adamant. Impartial, since he did not know her, sympathetic for he heard the distress in her voice as she sought his guidance, he was nevertheless ruthless.

'You must see, my child, that this is God's hand stretched out to guide you. To marry the man you love would have been placing yourself outside the holy rites of our Church. The Great Shepherd did not want to lose one of His sheep and so He has sent this new infant to you to guide you back to the fold. You must go back to your husband, my child, for that is very plainly God's will.'

'But of course he would say that,' Peter argued long into the night. *'He has to say things like that. It's his duty to keep you a good Catholic. Why did you go to him, Leanora? In your heart, you know you belong to me. This is right. We two together are right. We belong. It is you with him that is wrong, wicked. You say you don't love him; that you've always hated and dreaded his love-making. What could be more wrong than that? You live a lie. We are the truth.'*

But she knew he would not convince her. She listened, hoping that he would, that by some miracle he could. But all the time, feverish, tearless, agonised as she heard his voice, she knew she must fight against him. 'I love you, I love you!' was all she could say to comfort him.

She booked her ticket back, making a most solemn vow beneath the Statue of Our Lady that she would not miss the plane. Without that vow, there would have been a thousand times when she might have torn up the ticket, weakened beyond endurance.

Now the last final goodbye was said; the last kiss exchanged; the agony of life without him had begun.

'I wish the plane would crash and kill me!' she thought, knowing that this, too, was a sin. But she did not care. Probably there were other people in the plane to whom life was immeasurably precious. She thought of the young couple, so obviously honeymooners beginning their life together. How cruel to want her own death more than their happiness! And poor Edith Hurst—so thrilled with the prospect of going to South Africa as nanny to the new baby. All her life she had longed to travel and had never had the chance until now. How selfish to wish the poor woman's dreams might never be realised. And the pretty stewardesses—love, romance, marriage awaiting them. But she could not care about them either. Nothing mattered but her own despair.

'Peter, don't leave me!'

But it was she, Leanora Carson, thirty-two years old, beautiful, passionate, pregnant; wife, mistress, mother; she, who had left him!

*   *   *

'Weather looks perfectly okay to me!' said Denise to the girl on her right. It had been Ann's idea to come on this wildly expensive holiday. Denise was the youngest of the trio, Janet the oldest at twenty-five; Denise herself twenty and Ann twenty-two. They were all three hairdressers who lived and worked in Camberley in Surrey. For three years they had shared a football coupon, just for the fun of it, never really expecting to come up with a win.

When the incredible, the near-impossible, happened and they won eighty thousand, five hundred pounds between them, they'd been stunned. All their friends and relations had offered advice as to how to spend, save or invest their winnings. Three months went by before they finally decided to take the advice of Denise's father and buy a hairdressing shop of their own.

'Why work for anyone else when you can be your own bosses,' he had said. 'You've got the capital and the know-how!'

So it was decided. But first they wanted a holiday—an exciting, different, foreign holiday. They spent their weekends poring over brochures. Cruises to the Bahamas and the Greek islands were rejected—Janet was always seasick! India and the Far East were rejected—Denise's mother had lived in Bombay as a girl and hated it! Europe wasn't far enough across the world. In the end they had settled for South Africa. Ann's uncle lived in Natal and it seemed to offer everything the three girls wanted. They would take the plane directly there, spend two months in South Africa and then make their way slowly home, stopping off at Nairobi, Cairo and Rome.

When finally the tickets were bought and the last plan made, the three girls had reached the peak of anticipation and excitement. Now, sitting back in the luxurious comfort of the big V.C.10, Rome behind them and Cairo ahead of them, they were too exhausted to be voluble. It was enough to sit quietly, drinking in the thrill of their first-ever flight; of the lunch they had been served of hors d'oeuvre, cold chicken and ham, fruit salad and cheeses and biscuits. They'd kept their tiny cartons of salt and pepper as souvenirs as well as the little individual packets of milk and sugar served with their after lunch coffee and now with their tea.

That they were finally actually on this holiday of a lifetime still seemed a little dream-like to all three. Each had been through and was past the tiny moments of regret at leaving behind families and boy friends. All three had boy friends but had decided this trip must be made without them.

'After all, Janet,' Ann, the practical one, had said, 'we just *might* meet someone we don't even know exists at this moment and fall madly in love with them. It would spoil it if we go already tied down!'

Denise agreed. Janet, who'd been going steady with her Allan longest of all, had been the hardest to convince.

'Even if you think you're sure you'll never love anyone else more, then this will be an additional proof!' Ann said persuasively.

But the actual moment of goodbye hadn't been easy for any of them. Now, however, they were beginning to recover from the sadness of partings. Janet had even remarked on the dark good looks of the second pilot, so her friends knew she was going to be okay.

They smiled at each other contentedly. 'The Three Musketeeresses' they chose to call themselves. They had always got along famously, Janet's quiet, practical nature balancing Denise's volatile, excitable character; Ann placid but always able to make them laugh, rounded off the trio.

'We must be the luckiest girls alive!' Ann said sighing in the fulness of contentment.

But the other two were not listening. They were staring across the aisle at the charming spectacle of the pensioners, the old lady with her head on the old man's shoulder and their hands clasped tightly together.

'That,' whispered Janet delightedly, 'is what I call love!'

Harold and Elsie Curry were quite unaware of the glances of the three girls or their comments. They were remembering the many long years of hard work and the sacrifices they had made in order to achieve this—their life's ambition. They were now, at long, long last, on their way to see their daughter, Celia, again and the three grandchildren they had never met.

They could have gone years ago but bouts of bad luck had seemed to dog their lives. Harold had been made redundant and had been out of work for a two-year stretch which had forced them to draw heavily on their savings, although Elsie Curry continued with her own job as a milliner right up to her retirement and even then she had continued to take in sewing to help replace the lost savings.

Harold had managed at last to get another job but a severe attack of pneumonia made it impossible for him to continue with outdoor work. He'd worked as hard as his health would permit, doing free-lance interior decorating, although naturally this had not been as steady or lucrative as was his former employment with a building firm.

But both Harold Curry and his wife had been as firmly united in their resolve to visit Celia in South Africa as they were united in all other things. Theirs had been a perfect marriage, despite the set-backs and hardships. Celia, their clever, pretty daughter, had been a credit to them at school and university where she had met the young South African pilot she was eventually to marry.

It had broken their hearts to know she would be going to live on the other side of the world, but they never let her know this. They liked and approved of her young man and, certain that she loved him, encouraged the romance. They wanted her to be as happy as they themselves had been.

The births of their three grandchildren had brought inevitably a mixture of pain and pleasure. Celia sent photographs and every Christmas she sent tapes of the children talking to their grandparents. They wrote letters, sent gifts, kept in touch. But it wasn't the same as seeing, holding, hearing their own dear ones.

So the pennies and sixpences and, in good times, the shillings and pounds, had been faithfully and methodically put in the tin box in the wardrobe. The two ageing parents kept a silent but careful watch upon rising costs and hoped that they would one day be able to afford those precious air tickets.

On Harold's sixty-eighth birthday, they had reached their target. Elsie put away her needlework box; Harold took down his interior decorator's notice from the front room window; they took the bus into town and walked into the first travel agency they saw and booked their seats on the first flight to South Africa. They paid for their tickets in cash—counting out the pounds, shillings and pence. They sent an airmail letter to Celia, telling her to expect them. Elsie still had in her brown plastic handbag, Celia's reply: *Wonderful, wonderful news. Longing to see you both. Will all be at the airport to meet you!*

'Quite comfy, dear?' Harold had just asked his wife. But he knew her too well to take her assent for fact.

'There's nothing to be afraid of, Elsie luv. These big planes are as safe as buses. Why, they make trips like this a dozen times a day.'

She smiled at him reassuringly.

'I'm only afraid we shan't get to see Celia and the children. I'm not afraid of dying, Harold—not so long as I'm with you.'

That was when he took her hand, knowing

38

that it was true for him, too—dying didn't matter so long as they went together.

She put her head on his shoulder and he stroked the back of her hand. He never noticed that it had become gnarled and creased with age; that the skin was discoloured with brown spots and the veins enlarged. He knew only that he was holding hands with his girl, his Elsie, the way he always had and please God, the way he always would till the day he died.

* * *

The Honourable Sarah Finnon-Waters pushed the plastic tray away from her with a gesture of nervous irritability.

'Ugh! Tea!' she said for the second time in her high-pitched, upper-class voice. 'Revolting stuff!'

Her round, soft baby face was creased into a frown of discontent. The enormous violet-blue eyes, heavily darkened with mascara and outlined with thick false eyelashes, turned to the man beside her. She thought he looked perfectly horrible in that terrible lounge suit. It had struck her as funny when she'd seen it at the airport but now it had begun to annoy her. Conventional clothes didn't suit him. He looked his best in real mod gear. He had a smashing pair of pink kid boots which matched his favourite pink shirt. That was the kind of gear Larry looked good in. He was a fabulous dresser—really cared about his clothes. She liked him best in those black velvet matador pants with the lace-up flies and the white organdie frilled shirt.

She sighed.

It was hell having to pretend like this. Of course, Larry was right and they couldn't draw attention to themselves by the clothes they wore for the trip. But she hated the ghastly tweed suit she had on—reminded her too much of St Agnes' Sunday best. It was, in fact, a relic of schooldays, discarded six months ago when she'd finally talked Mummy into letting her leave school. Just as well Nanny hadn't given it to the jumble sale after all. Sarah couldn't think why Nanny kept anything so positively *ancient* hanging in mothballs in the spare room cupboard.

'It's a Harris Tweed, Miss Sarah, and there's years of good wear in it yet. I'll not throw it away.'

Poor, silly old Nanny. How she abominated fashion! Abomination was her favourite word. She abominated everything, from Sarah's mini skirts and false eyelashes and long hair to all the young men she brought home from art school. Poor old Nanny. If she thought those kids abominable, no wonder she nearly passed out when she met Larry. Pop music was anathema to Nanny. Daddy and Mummy tolerated it because they liked to think of

40

themselves as modern, progressive, liberal parents. Liberal, indeed! When it had come to the crunch, they'd been as old fashioned as the Victorians.

'Marry him, Sarah? Over my dead body. The boy's a hippy! I absolutely forbid it.' So much for liberal Daddy.

'Can't you see he's after your *money*, Sarah? For goodness' sake, child, come to your senses. A fortune hunter!' So much for with-it Mummy.

Neither seemed to appreciate that she *loved* Larry. Out came all the old clichés—too young to know your own mind; never should have let you leave school; drug addict; social climber . . . forbid it, forbid it, forbid it . . . until she thought she'd go crazy. Stop your allowance . . . not our class . . . common, vulgar, dirty . . .

It didn't seem to count that Larry was making a great deal of money; that he'd already had two records in the top twenty; it didn't matter that he was famous in the pop world even if *they'd* never heard of him. Underneath all the hypocritical pretence at being up-to-date, they were as old fashioned as the dinosaur. What did it matter whether she was an 'Honourable' or not? No one who was anyone cared about titles these days. In fact, Larry and the group all ragged her about it; made her feel inferior rather than superior. Why couldn't her parents see that that sort of thing was completely out-dated? What mattered was that she and Larry were crazy about one another. All her friends thought she was the luckiest girl alive and so she was, to have Larry Bell—the Larry Bell—in love with her. Why, he'd even agreed to marry her.

'Marriage is for the morons!' Larry had always maintained. But when he realised he might lose her if he didn't marry her, he'd allowed her to talk him into it.

'Daddy has threatened to have me made a ward of court. If that happens, Larry, they'll drag me home and I'll *have* to go. But if we get married and I can get pregnant, then my parents might come round to the idea. They're always preaching respectability. Well, they won't want me pregnant and *un*married, will they?'

If only she weren't so *young*. She might have reached the age of consent—which Larry said was damn lucky or he could go to prison!—but she still couldn't marry without her parents' permission and they could *make* her go home. If they forbade her to see Larry he'd find another girl, and who could blame him? There were hundreds of fans who'd be only too willing to step into her shoes.

Larry didn't take lightly to the idea of marriage. He couldn't see the point of it. It only made everything more difficult when it came to the crunch—and as far as he could see, most marriages came to the crunch sooner or later. Divorce was an unpleasant way out of the mess.

But Sarah had finally talked him round. Gretna Green would be a giggle—and when it did hit the papers, which it was bound to do in the end—it would make good publicity for Larry. All the world loved a lover.

But he had delayed a day too long. Daddy had twigged what was in the wind and they had a frantic last-minute rush to change their plans. Fortunately, Sarah's cousin, Susan Handley-Smith, had been willing to lend her passport; and the two were enough alike for Sarah to get away with it. Larry bought one in the name of Henry Bard, clerk, aged twenty-six. Hence the old-fashioned suit and, far worse, the short hair. Sarah had thought his long fair curls were fabulous and this new Larry was somehow off-putting. He had none of the glamour and colour of her own top-of-the-pops boy. Looking at him like this, she felt uneasy and very much in need of another drink.

'Tea!' she said again in a disgusted voice. 'What a drag!'

Larry scowled. Sarah had done nothing but criticise him since she'd first caught sight of him at the airport. He knew only too well that he looked a complete idiot but it was for *her* sake. The trouble with Sarah was she was damned spoilt. A spoilt little rich girl. Always had everything she wanted. In a way, he'd been flattered by the knowledge that a girl like her wanted him, Larry Bell, docker's son who'd grown up in the slums of Liverpool. With her education and background, she could have been going round with a lord. In fact, her father was one! It had been quite a triumph when he'd finally got Sarah to stay the night with him in his pad in Chelsea. But she turned out not so different after all from the other girls—going all romantic and soppy and talking about love all the time. Well, he'd taught her a thing or two and underneath all the la-di-dah nonsense, she'd turned out to be quite a hot little number. But marriage—well, that hadn't been in Larry's books at all. He'd fallen in with the Gretna Green idea because it sounded a bit of a lark and, as Sarah said, could make good publicity, seeing who she was and who he was. They'd make a packet selling their side of the story to the Sundays. And there was always divorce ...

But now he was in a good deal deeper than he'd wanted. He must have been pretty high agreeing to this crazy idea—Sarah's, of course. She was a crazy kid. She didn't seem to care she could get jugged for using someone else's passport. Her attitude had presented a kind of challenge to him—if she dared go through with it, he'd look pretty chicken if he backed out—and all his friends were in on the deal. Surprisingly, they backed Sarah's plans in exactly the same spur-of-the-moment way they backed any new idea flung into the group—a swim in Trafalgar Square fountain; a ton-up down the M1 on a foggy night; an LSD trip. It was all kicks to keep them amused and this would be a good one. They'd all change gear— wear their squarest clothes and turn up looking like a Sunday-school outing to see Larry and Sarah off at the airport.

The ideas got crazier than ever. Some guy produced Henry Bard's passport for Larry. Another telephoned the travel agency and booked their tickets. Until then, neither he nor Sarah had the vaguest idea where they'd fly to.

'Why South Africa?' he'd asked, not yet really with the mood.

'Why not?' they shouted back. He couldn't think of an answer.

Sarah had gone home to put up a smoke-screen of compliance with her family's wishes. She'd spent the night looking out suitable gear and packing. Larry and his gang continued the party without her. It got smokier, drunker, noisier. By four a.m. they had him rigged up to look as they imagined Henry Bard, clerk, of 15, Surbiton Avenue, would turn up for a plane trip to South Africa. They got him into the first barber's to open on their way to the airport. They forgot their intention to change clothes themselves. No one was sober enough to remember it except Larry and he was nearly asleep on his feet.

If the gang hadn't been with them, Larry might never have turned up at the airport.

45

Sarah was already there, bright, fresh but looking ghastly in the St Trinian's outfit, though as determined as ever. She took over management with the easy assumption of her class that her orders would automatically be carried out. The gang dispersed. Larry was made to drink two cups of black coffee to sober him up. Sarah was perfectly calm and even the news in the paper that 'Daddy's done it—made me a ward of court!' didn't scare her, or at least as far as Larry could see. It merely seemed to spur her on to outwit her father. He was forced to admit she was pretty cool. She had guts. More than he had right now. He felt sick thinking that in a moment or two, he was going to present that fake passport.

But there was no trouble. They passed through the barrier without a hitch. It had all been *too* easy. Susan Smith and Henry Bard were now aboard the V.C.10 and with the exception of the gang, not a soul in the world knew who they really were. Anonymity was what they wanted, of course, but having got it, Larry found himself deeply depressed at the loss of his famous identity. He'd striven too long and too hard to get recognised to enjoy this nonentity. All very well for Sarah, who'd been 'someone' all her life. It was not so long ago that Larry had been nothing more than a grubby docker's kid. Becoming Larry Bell, pop star, with all the resulting publicity and recognition wherever he went, his innermost needs realised in a way Sarah would never understand. It wasn't just the money—though God knew that counted—but he liked to have the kids raving hysterically when he got on stage; he liked walking into a West End restaurant and having the waiters rush to get him a good table; to see the mink-coated matrons who once wouldn't have given him the time of day, ogle and whisper about him. Fame got a chap respect and that snooty stewardess might be a bit more forthcoming if she knew who he really was. Fame bust the class barrier. It opened all doors, and he wasn't going to stay plain Henry Bard a moment longer than he had to.

He looked at Sarah resentfully. 'Shut up, can't you?' he said. 'I want to get some sleep.'

He closed his eyes; felt her hand close over his but ignored it. He guessed those enormous violet-blue eyes of hers would be staring at him reproachfully but he couldn't care less. She'd got him into this. Time she realised he was doing her a favour, risking a hell of a lot for her sake. And why? *Did he really love her?* Did he honestly want to be *married* to her? Okay, so he needed her. A girl of her class did something for him—provided him with something he couldn't get any other way. He hadn't worked it out but he knew he wasn't willing to give her up just because 'Daddy' thought he wasn't good enough. He'd show 'Daddy' who held the whip hand. Ward of court, indeed.

Drunk now with fatigue and the plane's steady droning, Larry fell into the deep unconsciousness of sleep.

CHAPTER THREE

Kennedy Maxwell's fingers tightened round the small gun now in his right-hand jacket pocket. For several years now it had been his practice to carry this little weapon with him, but he had never yet had occasion to use it. His wife, Nancy, had been scared by the implications of his carrying firearms. He'd never quite succeeded in persuading her it was just a very simple precaution 'in case' he met up with trouble.

He loved his wife very dearly. When he'd married her soon after her graduation from college, she'd been the prettiest thing he'd ever set eyes on—and intelligent, too. Now, after close on twenty years of married life, she was still remarkably attractive and his love for her had grown rather than diminished with the passage of time. She had made him a wonderful partner in every way; had helped him up the ladder by her grace and charm and sure-fire success as a hostess. And she had been a good mother. Her only fault, if you could call it a fault, was her susceptibility to

48

emotionalism in their private life. In public she never failed to appear cool, calm and reasonable. But as far as their personal relationship was concerned, Nancy could be as stupidly illogical and unreasonable as any other woman. She worried over the silliest things—his health, which was normally excellent, his physical safety, which had never yet been in jeopardy except for the couple of years he'd spent in Korea; his inability to look after himself if she were not there to 'mother' him.

Bruce Mallory had done a great deal to allay these notions of Nancy's. The young Californian's unquestionable loyalty and affection for her husband was a great reassurance to her. She saw Bruce not just as a highly efficient personal assistant, but as a bodyguard, too. The growing violence in the States had unnerved her and she was forever in fear that some half-crazed fool might try to assassinate him, though Maxwell had tried on innumerable occasions to point out that he wasn't important enough for anyone to want to bump him off! But that was Nancy and he'd had to accept this quirk—the more exaggerated since the assassination of his name-sake, President Kennedy.

It partly worried, partly amused this tall, grey-haired diplomat that a woman as intelligent and educated as his wife could possibly find an assocation between himself and an ex-President—but she'd managed to cook up a reason for her fears—that an ignorant foreigner might think he belonged to the Kennedy family! He'd tried not to laugh, knowing how worried she was. It was really to please her he had bought the gun but it had had the opposite effect. Now, illogically, she took it for granted that he would not have done so had he, himself, felt he was in no danger.

Maxwell sighed uneasily. If Nancy ever got to hear about this hi-jacking nonsense! If the men got away with it, it would be bound to cause quite a bit of publicity and Nancy would be out of her mind with worry. She knew his schedule, knew that he was due out of London Airport this morning for the Cairo talks and she would have him mentally dead and buried before he could get a wire off to reassure her!

Not that he really believed that there was any real danger. There *had* been an increasing number of planes successfully hi-jacked in recent months but as far as he knew, never a commercial British plane. The British crew would surely get on top of the situation.

He turned to his young companion.

'*You* don't think they'll get away with it, do you, Bruce?' he voiced his thoughts in an undertone.

Bruce Mallory shrugged.

'Could do!' he whispered back. 'I've been trying to fathom who those guys are. I seem to recall seeing a picture somewhere of the one sitting in front of you. Got a name like the Elephant Boy, Sabu.'

His hazel eyes suddenly brightened with excitement.

'I've got it, Sabuto. Nigerian guy. Got slung out last year when the Obburi tribe took over their State. Do you remember him? No one's heard much about him since. He's the eldest son of one of the chieftains.'

Kennedy Maxwell digested this information with misgivings. It was just like Bruce to have the necessary facts at his fingertips. He seldom forgot a face or a place or a person of importance. Sometimes Maxwell wondered how any human's memory could store such a fantastic amount of data. It was this retentive memory of Bruce's which helped to make him such a good p.a. It was a help, too, that he had no ties, though Nancy was always trying to marry him off to one of her eligible friends. 'He *ought* to be married' was one of Nancy's continual comments. Maxwell had gathered that the 'ought' referred to Bruce's 'husband and father potential'. In Nancy's view, Bruce was not a born bachelor.

Maxwell knew, of course, that Bruce had already been married once, ten years ago. His young wife had died giving birth to their first child which, also, had not survived. Bruce's reluctance ever to talk about his double tragedy convinced Maxwell and Nancy that it had been a very serious blow to him. Not that Bruce ever moped—far from it. He was a dab hand at all the parties, attracting all the unattached females in sight; and the attached ones, too, though he never became too involved. He was quite exceptionally attractive to women of all ages but it had not seemed to make him conceited. Maxwell had the impression that Bruce didn't care whether he attracted or not and this was, in fact, one of the main reasons females chased him. Bruce's indifference combined with his extreme good looks and easy, natural charm, presented an instant challenge. Maxwell was as familiar as Bruce himself must be with that look the pretty young stewardess had given him—the interested look, Maxwell called it when he ribbed his young assistant.

Now he hoped that the girl was as cool and imperturbable as she was pretty. It wasn't going to help this situation if anyone panicked. He wondered how many other passengers in the plane had been informed of the true situation. Bearing in mind the soothing message put over the tannoy, he doubted if many knew of the predicament they were in.

Bruce had taken one of the pamphlets out of the pocket of the seat in front of him and was studying a map. He jabbed a finger over Egypt.

'That's Cairo, where we should be heading!' he said, still keeping his voice low. 'Judging by the position of the sun, I'd say we were in fact heading south, here . . .' and he pointed again.

Maxwell's eyebrows shot up.

'That's across the Sahara!'

Bruce nodded.

'My bet is we're making for somewhere in Nigeria. Can't say I like the look of things, sir!'

The men were on long-standing friendly terms. Bruce usually only used the 'sir' on official duty. His unconscious choice of the word now doubled Maxwell Kennedy's growing anxiety. It was as if Bruce were indicating that this was not for fun.

'Ring for that stewardess of yours,' he said, attempting a smile. 'Ask her for our flying speed. If we know that, we can work out very roughly where we are. Get the exact time we left Rome, too.'

Bruce was glad now of the opening he'd given himself to buzz the stewardess. If the men in front were listening, and he was pretty sure they were, they'd assume he was just trying to get the girl's attention, to continue his flirtation with her.

How pretty she was! he thought as she came smoothly up the aisle towards him. No, not pretty, exactly, but she sure was attractive.

'Yes, sir?'

He liked her English accent, too. He grinned.

'You never did tell me your name,' he said, using the loud, brash voice favoured by so

53

many American tourists. 'It's not against the regulations to tell me who you are, is it?'

Although Eve was well aware that this conversation was for the benefit of any eavesdropper, she still flushed.

'No, sir, it's not against the rules. I'm Eve Cunningham.'

'Mrs or Miss?'

'Miss!'

'Well, that's fine, honey. What say you and I go some place when we get to Cairo? Can't be too soon for me. Say, how fast does this old jalopy travel? How fast you reckon we're flying?'

Eve told him. She was beginning to understand now the drift of his conversation.

'And we left Rome around lunch-time, was it?'

Eve gave him the exact time.

'Well then, I reckon we'll be home and dry by five. Right, honey? Now don't go away, beautiful. I've a whole heap more questions. I want you to lean right over here and see this map. I want you to show me just where Cairo is. I sure as hell can't find it!'

As she leant towards him, Bruce drew a dark pencil line over the map. He drew a small cross and said:

'If that's Cairo, honey, I guess we'll be about here, right?'

She understood and nodded. Bruce's long, tapering finger was tracing a line southeast towards Nigeria. He was indicating where he thought they were heading.

'Anything else, sir?'

He looked up, the serious expression of his eyes giving way once more to laughter.

'Well, I can't rightly think up any other reason to detain you, honey, but I will. You haven't said you'll accept my invitation yet. You just go think about it. I reckon you and me would hit it off real swell.'

Not sure whether to laugh or frown, Eve left him and returned to the galley. She reported the conversation to Mary-Lou.

'I know he's acting a part,' she said, 'but all the time I'm sure he's very much aware of the seriousness of the position. I know it's silly, Mary-Lou, but I'm glad we've got him on board. I think he's intelligent. If anyone is going to help us out of this mess, it'll be him.'

'Well, well, well!' Mary-Lou drawled, *sotto voce*. 'Can't say I've known you show this much interest before, darling. Still, I do agree he's dishy—even if this isn't the appropriate time to be thinking of such trifling matters!'

Eve drew a deep breath.

'Looks like we'll be spending the night in Nigeria!' she said. 'If he's right . . . and if we don't run out of fuel before we get there . . .'

'Just so long as we don't land in the Sahara!' Mary-Lou rejoined, laughing.

Both girls were finding it easier to take the situation light-heartedly. To admit to each

55

other their inner fears would only add to the reality for their cause.

They were disturbed by the appearance of the mother of the sick girl. As first they thought she was making for the toilet but she paused just inside the curtained entrance to the galley and said:

'Please, could I have a word with you?'

Her grey hair was dishevelled, her face and eyes both revealing acute nervous anxiety.

'It's my daughter, Jennifer,' she said, addressing her remarks to Eve. 'I'm afraid I'll have to ask you if you could get a message through somehow to the airport authorities at Cairo and ask them to have an ambulance ready to take her straight to hospital.'

The words came out with a rush. Eve sensed the woman was near breakdown and with calm professionalism, sat her down on Mary-Lou's tip-up seat.

'Try not to worry, Mrs James,' she said soothingly. This was obviously not the time to tell her they wouldn't be landing at Cairo the way things were shaping. 'Maybe I can help your daughter. Can you give me some idea what is wrong?'

She was puzzled. If the girl needed a fix why didn't she give herself one in the loo? Did her parents know the truth? What would happen when they finally realised there would be no landing at Cairo!

The whole sad story of Jennifer came

56

pouring out of Mrs James. Jennifer was on heroin. That was why her parents were taking her for an indefinite holiday to South Africa. They wanted her to be right away from the dreadful crowd she'd been mixing with, and who had supplied her with the stuff. Her parents managed to persuade her a few months ago, to go into a private nursing home and take the cure, but Jennifer had discharged herself halfway through. She'd begun drugging again. In desperation they'd planned this trip. Jennifer had agreed to go.

She seemed to be leaving the stuff alone before they left home, said she could manage the journey without it. They'd contacted a relative in Cape Town who'd made arrangements for Jennifer to go straight to hospital as soon as they arrived. They'd been sure that she was better and off drugs already. For a whole week she hadn't been out with the gang!

'But she must have been still taking it at home, though she swore on her oath that she was not!' the frantic mother told Eve. 'We didn't realise. I did think she might have hidden some of the horrible stuff somewhere in her luggage, knowing she wouldn't have any contacts to get supplies from in Cape Town, so at the last minute I swapped suitcases. I'd bought her a second set of everything she'd need for the journey and last night I just put *her* case on the bonfire. Jennifer didn't know.

I'd bought identical cases, you see. I thought it was for the best. I didn't want her to have any kind of supplies she could start on again out there. Now she's suffering and I don't know what to do.'

Eve caught Mary-Lou's eye and bit her lip. What could be done? They had morphine on board but Mrs James had referred to a different drug. Could they be mixed? *Should* they be mixed? Would it help the girl? Eve simply did not know the answer and the radios were out of action—they couldn't radio back for medical advice.

Mrs James was clutching her arm. 'You must help me. I must do something. It's my fault she has nothing to take now. But I didn't realise. I . . .'

'I could produce some sleeping pills,' Eve suggested quickly. 'They might knock her out for a while.'

'But, Eve, if we're not landing at . . .' Mary-Lou broke off in mid sentence. The woman might very well become hysterical if she knew the seriousness of the situation on board. Better she did not know there would very likely be no Cairo, no ambulance. As to whether they could obtain medical help 'somewhere in Nigeria', she very much doubted it.

But Eve was already unlocking the medicine chest, searching for the sleeping pills. Fortunately, the distraught woman seemed not to have grasped Mary-Lou's meaning.

When she left them alone Eve shook her head.

'This is really going to complicate things, Mary-Lou. If that James girl gets unruly— throws a fit or something—she'll unsettle the other passengers, not to mention the three African gentlemen. They might opt to silence her in their own way and . . .'

'There's John coming down with the tea cups,' Mary-Lou broke in. 'Perhaps he'll have some better news for us.'

But the news was far from good. Bob was still heading south at gunpoint, John told them. He had little doubt that the Nigerian would shoot without the slightest compunction if he was disobeyed. The man seemed to know enough about flying to check on Bob's vector, height, fuel capacity. Their only hope lay in the fact that Cairo would have lost radar contact and might begin to worry about them.

'Trouble is,' John said, 'we were over the sea when radio contact was lost. The assumption could well be that we've gone down in the drink. Not that they will do anything about us until we're actually over-due and that won't be for another half hour.'

Eve told him that the Americans had a gun.

John Wilson nodded approvingly.

'Could be a help. I'll find a way to let Bob know. But for the time being Bob says we should obey orders. Naturally he's got to think

59

of the passengers' safety and with two machine-guns on board—well . . .'

'There are eight of us against three of them,' Eve said thoughtfully. 'And some of the other passengers might be able to back up any plan we could devise for rushing the two up front.'

'You can't count on Bob or Jimmy—not with a gun behind them. And what can the rest of you do, two against two machine-guns?' John said doubtfully.

'Whichever of the two Americans has the gun could shoot both men before they could even get their machine-guns ready,' Eve argued. 'Surely it's worth a chance, John?'

He grimaced.

'They already have their machine-guns ready—on their laps covered by a coat. I noticed as I came past. Anyway, Eve, it still leaves the third man with his gun on Bob and Jimmy.'

'But if he did shoot them, who'd fly the plane?' Eve countered. 'He wouldn't dare do it.'

John sighed.

'I'm afraid he would. He informed us just now and I don't think he was bluffing—that he's an experienced pilot. Granted he hasn't flown anything as big as this but he's flown smaller planes and I don't doubt he could manage this one at a pinch. No, it looks like stalemate for the moment. But cheer up. I think Bob may be hatching an idea. He's been hinting at having something up his sleeve. I'll keep you posted. I came back just to make sure you were both okay.'

He squeezed Mary-Lou's hand, his eyes smiling but not really masking his anxiety for her.

She told him quickly and briefly about the James girl. He looked concerned and promised to let Bob know what was up.

'Keep her quiet, for God's sake,' he said. 'We don't want to panic the bastards into using those guns! Now give me a couple of packs of cigarettes. That was my excuse for coming back here. And by the way, our black companion goes by the name of Engarri. He's a Nigerian from the Mabu tribe—anti the Obburri government. Oh, well, happy days, girls! Keep smiling.'

But Mary-Lou could no longer smile. She looked at Eve with the fear showing for the first time.

'Do you think we'll get out of this—alive?' she asked the older girl tentatively.

Eve managed a laugh.

'But of course. Why on earth not, if we do as they say? There's nothing to be gained by killing us all off.'

'But when we've landed—wherever it is they want us to land,' Mary-Lou persisted. 'What else will we be then but thirty-four hindrances?'

Eve swallowed her own fears and said very firmly indeed:

'Don't be silly, Mary-Lou. It hasn't happened yet and it won't happen now. Besides, Bob'll think up something—you'll see. Now get those tea trays collected and washed up. We'll be wanting them for supper soon.'

The younger girl reacted at once to Eve's authority. As Eve had guessed, she was much happier when she had something to do.

*   *   *

Chris Barlow took his young wife's hand in his and held it tightly. She gave him a radiant smile from beneath the curtain of corn-gold hair. This habit of smiling sideways through her hair always produced the exact same physical effect upon him, making him want her, urgently and immediately, regardless of time or place or even of how recently he had just made love to her.

He was slightly shocked at himself that even now, with the pink slip of paper screwed up in his hand, warning him of the serious situation that existed on board—a situation which could put all their lives in jeopardy—he was able to let the thought of sex with Liz overrule any other consideration. If they were all going to die, then he wanted to make love to Liz once more at least before life came to an end!

'Christopher John Barlow, you shock me!'

he told himself, but at the same time he had begun to stroke the back of Liz's hand and then to intertwine his fingers with hers so that their two palms touched at all possible points of contact. While he did this he watched her face, eager to see the slow flush of colour rise in her cheeks, to hear her quickened breath and to know he had made her physically aware of him.

'I'll tell her we're in danger in a minute,' he thought. But when he spoke it was only to say breathlessly:

'I want you terribly, darling!'

'Me, too!' she whispered back, leaning the weight of her slim young body against his arm.

But he knew he wasn't going to be able to make love to her for hours yet. South Africa and the double room he'd booked for their honeymoon was still a hell of a long way off— if they ever got there at all . . .

His thoughts went back to last night at the Skyways Hotel—their wedding night. Both had been a little afraid that it would prove something of an anti-climax. After all, they had been making love in Chris' London flat for the last six months so it wasn't a question of 'the first time'. Yet curiously, it had seemed like the first time. Liz had been so different.

In the past, when they'd never been completely sure whether his flat mate might come marching in, Liz had been shy, nervous; willing enough to make love but more to please him than herself. He'd been ignorant enough to believe he had everything he wanted. He was so much in love with her that their rather hurried, unsatisfactory love-making had been pushed to the back of his mind. When he had thought about it at all, it was with the comfortable thought that everyone said sex improved with time.

It certainly improved with marriage, he told himself now. Last night the rather cool, restrained young girl had become as wildly passionate as himself. He'd been surprised—wonderfully so. Liz said it was because she felt 'safe' now, though he couldn't really see why the civil ceremony should have had this extraordinary effect upon a girl's nature. It wasn't as if she'd been afraid of having a baby before—they'd both known she was safe enough on the pill. But he didn't waste time wondering about her transformation. He'd been too busy enjoying it!

Liz was twenty-three. She had a good job as secretary to a publisher and made herself so indispensable to her boss that he'd been perfectly willing to accept Liz's terms for staying on with the firm after her marriage—i.e. a month off for her honeymoon and when she did return, no overtime and no Saturdays. He'd even thrown in a two-pound-a-week rise, which would come in very useful since they'd put down the key money for a new flat and, what with the crazy expense of this honeymoon, had little left with which to furnish it.

'Who cares about furniture,' Liz had said when they were trying to make up their minds whether to scrap the honeymoon altogether or blow the rest of their savings. 'Our honeymoon will be something to remember all our lives, Chris. Besides, darling, I've always longed and longed to go there. Please, darling!'

He hadn't cared where he went so long as he was with her. It could have been Timbuctoo or the Old Kent Road for all he cared. But gradually he'd come round to sharing some of her excitement. Boarding the plane at Heathrow this morning, he'd felt in his bones that Liz was right—this was going to be something to remember always. The whole long month ahead of them was a marvellous holiday to look forward to—far away from anyone in the world who knew them. They'd be totally and completely alone—the two of them.

If they ever arrived . . .

Chris was forced back to reality. He'd noticed the pilot passing him on his way to the stewardesses' galley, and his return a short while after. The man's face had looked anxious. Chris wished someone would tell him exactly what was going on. Whatever it was, it was something he'd be able to tell the chaps about when he got back to the bank. They'd all got sick and tired of hearing old Jeffries' story of how he'd been held up at gunpoint at the branch where he'd worked previously. The poor old devil had lived off that story for years. Chris must watch he didn't bore everyone telling them this adventure once too often.

If he ever got back to tell them at all . . .

'Liz!' His voice was different now, underlined with seriousness. 'Things aren't going too smoothly, I'm afraid. There's a bit of trouble on board!'

He told her the little he knew and felt her fingers tighten round his.

'Don't be scared, darling!' he said. 'I expect the crew will cope okay. Just thought I'd let you know what was in the wind.'

Liz Barlow trod firmly on the quiver of fear that ran through her. She felt instinctively that they were in danger, despite Chris' reassurances.

'At least I'm with Chris!' she thought. 'So long as I'm with Chris, I don't mind dying!'

But of course, she did mind. Now, more than at any other time in her whole life, she wanted to live. She wanted to go on living and loving Chris for years and years and years. She wanted to have his children and take care of him and love him and love him. She'd wasted twenty-three years of life not loving him and she wanted to catch up for all the lost time. In a strange kind of way, she felt she had only been born last night. She'd become a new person, which was true in a way. Liz Matthews had become Mrs Christopher Barlow. Girl had become woman. Spinster had become wife.

'Oh, *darling!*' she said, her voice husky. 'I *do* love you!'

Chris smiled, happy, again. In the midst of possible death and disaster, all Liz could think of was that she loved him. It was immensely flattering.

'I love you, too!'

She smiled at him and he smiled back. She loved the way his eyes crinkled at the corners when he laughed; the way his mouth, a little large and lopsided, turned upwards at the edges. She loved everything about him—the crisp wiry hair at the nape of his neck, the firm jaw, the angular face and the heavy dark eyebrows which made him look years older than the twenty-three he could claim. She could well understand the bank manager's remark that Christopher was a steady young man who'd go places. He was much more mature than most young men of his age, but then he'd had to be since he was an orphan and had been brought up in a Home with no relatives to back him or help him. She pitied him his lonely childhood but at the same time, she relished the thought that she was all the family he had had. It somehow made him more dependent upon her and she liked the feeling. Not that he depended on her in the wrong way. He was strong minded and had a will of his own.

'Must have!' she told herself with a little quirk of her eyebrows. He'd persuaded her to sleep with him before marriage and she'd always sworn she'd stay a virgin until the day she wore a wedding ring. She'd never really found it very difficult to stick to these principles. The boy friends she had had before Chris had somehow failed to rouse more than the surface of the deep pools of passion that lay dormant and unknown to her. With Chris, everything had been different. Sex had taken on a new dimension and every hour spent with him was a battle between her desire and his, and her principles.

Now, looking at the past year in retrospect, she was astonished that she could have held out so long. Now it was all very different indeed—she thought it might even be possible that she wanted Chris more than he wanted her, or at any rate, as much. If there really was a possibility that they were going to die on this plane, she just wished it would be possible to die in the middle of love-making. She was a little shocked at herself and decided to tell Chris later how she felt and see if she shocked him. Maybe he was feeling the same way!

Her fingers tightened once more around his. How she loved this feeling of belonging; of being not two people but one. She didn't believe any two people could be as wonderfully happy and well suited as she and Chris. She was so sorry for all the other girls who weren't married to him. Take those three girls just in front of them. They were all quite pretty—to be fair, every bit as pretty as she was—and Chris might have met and married any one of them. The girl in the middle had the most beautiful hair—strawberry blonde, Liz thought the colour was called. Chris said he adored her own ordinary corn-coloured hair and it was true he never got tired of running his hands through it but he seemed to wear rose coloured spectacles where she, Liz, was concerned. She was secretly afraid that he might wake up one of these days and see her as she really was—just ordinarily attractive. Suppose he were to meet a girl like the one with the reddish hair and fall in love with her? How could she bear it? She knew that she could not. She hated the girl in front with an idiotic, if momentary, fury. She wondered if the girls were getting off at Cairo but remembered unhappily that she'd heard them talking about South Africa. Just so long as they weren't staying in the same hotel as herself and Chris!

She wondered if Chris would feel as jealous as she knew she could be, if she smiled at that handsome young pilot! Not that he was her type. Chris was her type and she wouldn't even look twice at the pilot in fact. But if she did smile at him, how would Chris feel?

She sighed. There was so much she still did not know about him even after all this time.

Somehow staying odd nights at his flat and never being sure whether that boy, Stephen, would come butting in, she'd never felt able to relax completely. There had even been times when she had felt actually resentful that Chris should want to put her in such a compromising position. She hadn't really enjoyed sex then— not the way it was last night. She knew that it was going to become even more wonderful. She almost wished now that they'd been married in church though it had seemed a bit silly until now, both of them being agnostics. Her mother had been disappointed. Poor old Mum had wanted a white wedding and all the trimmings. But with Dad dead and Mum so hard up and the expense and everything, they'd decided against it. Would she have felt more married if the ceremony had been in church?

Liz felt the pressure of Chris' arm against hers and knew that nothing could have made him more her husband than he was this very minute. How happy she was! How happy they were going to be! She wasn't frightened, and wasn't going to be frightened by any silly man with a gun. This was a British plane and even Mum said they were as safe as any plane could be.

She found herself wondering whether her mother and father could ever have been as much in love as she and Chris. She couldn't believe it, though Mum had gone grey in the

70

fortnight after Dad's death. She was only forty-two, too. Poor Mum. She pitied her the same way she pitied the three girls who weren't married to Chris and on their honeymoon. She drew a long deep sigh.

'Did you say something, darling?'

She smiled at her young husband lovingly, and shook her head. But bending closer so that no one should over-hear, she whispered:

'Only that I love you!'

And felt a great surge of longing as Chris dug his nails sharply into the soft palm of her hand.

CHAPTER FOUR

Bob Sinclair drew in his breath anxiously. In a minute or two he'd have to point out to the hi-jackers that they couldn't hope to make Nigeria on the amount of fuel left in No. 2 tank. Like it or not, they'd have to turn back— land at Tripoli probably.

He caught John's eye and saw the look of concern on his face. It was a hell of a position to be in. Lilian would be crazy with worry if she knew—and she would be bound to hear the worst sooner or later. He just hoped they'd land in time for him to get a wire off to say he was safe before the airport let her know they were overdue at Cairo. The way things were going, it didn't look as if he'd be successful. Cairo might even be in touch with London by now.

Over the years of marriage to a mainline pilot, Lilian had managed to learn to live with the fear of a plane disaster. When they'd first married, she'd worried herself stupid if he was five minutes late home or the weather was foggy or she heard about a plane crash on the radio. Now they'd both become realistic about the dangers. Statistically, his chances of survival were far higher than if he'd been driving a car every day, or even taking a train to work each morning. They had ceased years ago to discuss the various causes of air disasters. But, strangely, they had never once talked about Bob's plane being hi-jacked. In a way, it had its funny side—the one danger they hadn't foreseen!

He glanced down at the indicator and saw that No. 2 tank was dangerously low. They'd been due to refuel at Cairo and carried only a small surplus. He squared his shoulders and said to the man who called himself Engarri:

'Nigeria's out, I'm afraid. I've been checking the fuel supply. We've barely enough even if we turn back now, to make Tripoli.'

He felt a moment of real paralysing fear at the expression on the Nigerian's face. If ever a man looked murderous, he did. Then his expression changed to one of disbelief.

'You've fixed it up to look as if we're out of

fuel!' he accused Bob, jabbing the gun in his back. 'Stay on the course I gave you!'

He took a step backwards and without lowering his gun or taking his eyes off the three men, he opened the cockpit door and called to his two friends. One remained seated with his head so turned that he could watch all the passengers. The other joined Engarri in the cockpit. In a low-voiced, unintelligible dialect, Engarri informed his confederate of the situation.

'If you don't allow me to turn back at once, it'll be too late!' Bob repeated for good measure. He could see the second man hesitating. But the first was shaking his head, scowling.

'You will go on!' he ordered. 'We do not believe you about the fuel!'

Bob glanced quickly at John and back to the man behind him.

'I give you my word, we've only an hour's flying time at the very most on the fuel we have left. The indicator can't lie—you must know that. Have some sense, man, and work it out for yourself. If we go on like this we're going to come down in the Sahara!'

He was speaking absolutely truthfully and, he hoped, convincingly. But the two men merely shrugged their shoulders.

'You're crazy!' John cried out. 'You'll kill us all!'

'The Sahara's a hell of a big place,' Jimmy

put in. 'We might never be located. Do you want to die of thirst? I thought you wanted to get to Nigeria and start a revolution? You won't do that from a grave in the desert!'

The second man, Angorro, looked hesitant but Engarri, obviously the more important of the two, broke out once more in his dialect. Angorro shrugged and returned to his seat.

'My God!' Bob burst out. 'This is really serious. They can't mean it!'

'They can, you know!' John muttered. 'Must be out of their minds. Is it true—one hour to go?'

Bob nodded. He glanced down apprehensively at the fuel gauge. It was far, far too low ever to make Nigeria. It really looked as if it must be the Sahara and then God help them all! He wasn't even sure if he could land in the sand. Could he do it? And even if they got down safely, how would they survive?

He turned once more to address Engarri but the man was obviously disinclined to listen to any more arguments. His mind was made up and with the stubbornness of the stupid, he wasn't going to change it. He dealt Bob a painful blow on the shoulder with his gun butt.

'No more talk!' he said roughly. 'You talk, I use this!'

And he waved the gun at each of them in turn.

Various plans flitted through Bob's aching head. He could try altering course—but the sun was still blazing through the cockpit window and only a child could fail to notice if he turned the plane round. He wondered if he dared tackle the man behind him, risking the promised bullet in an attempt to overpower him. But it would still leave the two other men. He didn't give much for the chances of a safe landing anywhere if he, John and Jimmy were wiped out, not to mention the lives of his passengers.

Now, for the first time, he was fully aware of the fact that he was no longer in control of his plane. There wasn't even time enough left to get them back to Tripoli now. Every mile they flew south meant a longer journey back to safety.

He began to worry what the Nigerians would do when they finally accepted the fact that they were going to come down in the desert whether they wished it or not. Would they kill him? His one chance lay in the fact that they'd need him to get this old bus safely down. An inexperienced pilot wouldn't have a hope.

The minutes were ticking by. He saw the sweat on John's forehead and realised that he, too, was wringing wet. But it was he, the Captain, who was responsible for the lives of the thirty-four passengers. He couldn't even put a Mayday signal over the radio. The search planes wouldn't have a clue where to begin looking for them even if they did manage to land.

Somehow, the tension eased a little once they were past the point of no return. Now that there were no more decisions to make, he could concentrate on the landing. If the three hi-jackers dropped dead this minute he was still going to have to come down in the Sahara, so he might as well forget them for the time being and think about the real problems immediately ahead of him.

'I must inform the passengers we are shortly going to make a forced landing,' he said eventually, risking another blow from Engarri's gun. 'If I don't do this, many will be killed or injured. There will be a panic and I can't answer for your life or that of your friends in such a situation!'

Something in Bob's voice must have impressed the African with its sincerity. His eyes opened wide and for the first time, Bob saw fear in them.

'I warned you we were low on fuel!' he said quietly. 'I wasn't bluffing. Believe me, I'm not bluffing now. The last thing I want to do is scare my passengers.'

'It is the desert—below?'

Engarri's voice was several tones higher, laced now with growing fear.

Bob nodded. 'Miles and miles and miles of it. We'll be coming down in about ten minutes' time.'

The man's hand was shaking.

'You turn north. You go to Tripoli. At once. I command it!'

'Too late for that now!' Bob said dryly. But he turned the plane none the less. They would still be better off nearer to Tripoli than Nigeria!

His readiness to obey further confused the Nigerian. He called Angorro once again and the two voices became shrill with argument. Finally they went back to the cabin, leaving the cockpit unguarded.

'Phew!' Jimmy said, wiping his brow for the tenth time. 'I gather you were stating facts, Bob?'

' 'Fraid so. Put over a message to the passengers, Jim. Try to sound calm. You know, shoes off, false teeth out, spectacles off, hands over the backs of their necks and so on. No need to explain about the Nigerians at the moment. That can come later. Let's get them down safely first!'

Whilst Jimmy started broadcasting, John and Bob discussed how best to bring the plane down. There was no knowing yet what kind of terrain they'd find beneath them. Bob knew there were mountains in the Sahara, some even high enough to have snow on them for three months of the year! He just hoped they would find flat ground, even if it were sand.

The Nigerians did not reappear. John, going to the cockpit door, informed his captain that all three were following the emergency drill.

'They look scared out of their wits!' he said with a grin. 'Reckon I could take their guns off them without the slightest trouble!'

Bob raised his eyebrows.

'Bit risky. We don't want any shooting now. I'm down to ten thousand feet. Check with the girls, John. See they've got everything battened down that can be! And give our two young stewardesses a helping hand.'

He scribbled a message for John to give the Americans. It was to tell them to use the gun if they could during the confusion of the landing. The three male members of the crew would each tackle one of the Nigerians the moment the plane was down but any action they saw fit to take to overpower the men first, they could work out for themselves.

'But tell the rest of the passengers to sit tight and not to worry,' he added. 'Say I'm the best pilot that ever flew yet and they'll be okay! Good luck!'

'Five thousand feet!' John reported beside him. 'I can see the deck, Captain—sand, and sand and more sand. Looks fairly flat. Mountains south and east—high ones.'

Bob pushed forward the stick and the great V.C. 10 continued its flight down towards the shimmering expanse of sand below.

The most remarkable thing after the landing was the silence. The terrible roar of the engines had died away. No one spoke. Only the Americans moved. Standing up

78

swiftly, Kennedy Maxwell pointed his gun at the three revolutionaries still strapped in their seats.

Bob, opening the cockpit door, noticed at once that he had nothing more to fear from that quarter. The men were unresisting and Bruce Mallory was already quietly removing their guns. The landing had been miraculously easy on the hard dry sand. There was no danger of fire and no need for an emergency exit, he quickly informed Eve and Mary-Lou. One or two of the passengers sat up and began to unfasten their safety belts. Rows of shocked faces were turned expectantly towards Bob.

'I am your Captain, Bob Sinclair,' he said. His voice was hoarse but at least it sounded steady though his hands were still shaking. 'I would like you all to remain in your seats for a few minutes while we get organised. I'll ask the stewardesses to bring round free drinks—I'm sure you could all do with one and so could I!'

There was a murmur of voices. Someone congratulated him on the landing.

'As you know, we've just had to make an emergency landing, but I'm glad to say without mishap.'

It seemed a good time to inform them, whilst they were still in a state of shock, about the hi-jackers. Those near enough to see Mallory and Kennedy Maxwell with the machine-guns had already forgotten the landing and were staring with a mixture of apprehension and curiosity. He gave a brief run-down of events, concluding in a firm voice:

'As most of you can see, we now have the causes of our trouble well under control so no one is in any danger. Now, was anyone hurt in the landing? I'm afraid it was a pretty bumpy one.'

There was a babble of voices. A grey-haired woman lifted her hand and said in a quiet steady voice:

'I'm afraid my employer, Mrs Carson, has hurt her back!'

Bob glanced anxiously at the passenger in question. Leanora Carson was lying back in her seat, her eyes closed, her mouth twisted in pain.

He beckoned Eve to come and attend to her.

'Apart from Mrs Carson, everyone else is okay? Then we can count ourselves lucky. As you can see, we have come down in the desert. Don't let this frighten you. We have plenty of water on board and it's only a matter of time before the search planes locate us. But this may take a little while as our radios aren't functioning. So I think we should prepare to spend at least a night or two where we are. I'm very sorry indeed that you won't be able to make your destinations on time but I hope that you'll all be on your way before too long.'

The questions began now but he held up his hand for silence.

'In a minute or two I'll be available to answer any questions but first I want to finish what I have to say. We're lucky that the passenger load is only a third of our usual capacity. There should therefore be plenty of room for you all to stretch our fairly comfortably for the night. It can be extremely cold in the desert at night so the stewardesses will bring round as many blankets as we can supply. There's no reason why those of you who wish shouldn't disembark before dark, but if you do, watch out for the sun. The temperature is probably something like a hundred degrees in the shade! Also don't go far—we don't want to lose any of you. And don't try to leave until we've rigged up some way to get down, it's quite a long way.'

He could see Mary-Lou taking round the first tray of drinks. He badly needed a brandy but knew he'd have to wait a while.

'The next thing is food—we've quite a supply on board, probably more than we'll want but I'm sure you'll all agree with me that it would be a wise precaution not to eat *more* than we want this evening. Although, as I said, I've every hope that we'll be located quickly, we would be ill advised not to cover ourselves for a day or two, just in case. For the same reason, we'll go carefully with the water. Don't use the toilets. We'll dig a latrine a little way away from the 'plane. I'll be asking for volunteers in a minute. Don't wash, or if you

81

do, use the very minimum of water, and don't leave a tap running. You can smoke as much as you want—we've adequate supplies of tobacco on board and a fair amount of alcohol, though I don't advise too much drinking in this heat. Now my co-pilot, John Wilson, and I will be in the front seats if anyone has any questions. We'll do whatever we can to make things as pleasant as possible. Thank you for listening; thank you for behaving so very well during the landing; and thank you for taking this so calmly.'

'Before you go up front, Captain, what shall we do with this lot?' Bruce Mallory spoke quietly at his elbow.

Bob had temporarily forgotten the Nigerians. He met Bruce's grin with an answering smile.

'I honestly haven't a clue!' he said truthfully. 'I suppose we'd better lock them up somewhere.'

Kennedy Maxwell said:

'Pity I didn't shoot them!'

'We could put them in the luggage hold,' John suggested. 'There's plenty of rope back there. We could tie 'em up.'

Bob nodded. His legs were beginning to shake. The reaction to the strain of landing, by no means easy, was getting hold of him.

'We'll fix them!' Bruce Mallory said, noting the pallor of Bob's face. 'You go sit down and have a drink, you've earned it!'

'Try not to let the passengers get panicky!' Bob warned. 'Everyone's calm now and I don't want to upset them.'

Kennedy Maxwell walked up the cabin beside Bob. Eve came along with two brandies and reported to Bob she didn't think Mrs Carson was badly hurt. There didn't appear to be any bones broken. She disappeared again, cool and efficient, and left the two men together.

'I take it you think we might be here quite some time,' Maxwell said quietly. 'When did the radios go out of action?'

Bob glanced at his companion thoughtfully. Here, he thought gratefully, was a man who was going to be of inestimable value to him if they were as lost as he suspected. He felt instinctively that he could trust Maxwell. He said frankly:

'Could be a week—or longer!'

'Or for ever?'

The cool grey eyes met Bob's without flinching.

'Let's hope for the best,' Bob replied. 'They'll certainly search for us but will they search here? It's my bet they'll be out from Malta looking for oil slicks in the Med. I've been racking my brain but I can't think of one good reason why anyone should suspect we turned round in mid air and were heading for Nigeria!'

Kennedy Maxwell felt the first shiver of fear

run up his spine. It was worse than he'd thought.

'Could we be near a trade route? An oasis?'

'I just don't know, Mr Maxwell. In fact I know very little indeed about the Sahara other than that it's a bloody big place!'

'And mighty hot!'

They grinned at each other. Bob finished his brandy and felt better.

'I don't think it's advisable to say anything about being "lost" to the rest of the passengers for the time being. They've had enough shocks for one day. We'll save the rest for tomorrow.'

Kennedy stood up.

'Well, I'm glad we've got you for Skipper, Captain. Let me know if there's anything at all I can do.'

'One thing,' Bob said as the American began to move off. 'I think the passengers ought to have someone for spokesman. If you'd organise some kind of committee . . . ?'

He had no need to go on. Kennedy understood.

The trainer of the football team was waiting to talk to Bob. He introduced himself and said:

'My men all coloured. Used to heat. You all white people and will suffer very much. Plane get very hot in the sun. Not good. Everyone get ill from heat. Best sit outside in shade of the wings.'

Bob thanked him. It was a useful tip though, as he pointed out to the Kenyan, it was getting late in the day now. The sun would be going down in about ten minutes. Already it hung in a great fiery ball on the edge of the western horizon. The sky was a canvas of fantastic orange, red and gold streaks. A group of passengers were admiring the sunset.

Chris Barlow was next in line to see Bob. He wanted merely to offer his services should Bob require them in dealing with the captive Nigerians.

'Or if I can help in any other way, I will,' he said. 'I'm pretty fit—and strong, too.'

Bob thanked him and referred him to Kennedy Maxwell.

Jimmy came through from the cockpit, reporting that he couldn't see much hope of repairing the radios. The contact points were badly damaged but he couldn't tell until he stripped them how much internal damage had been done.

'I'll get working on it right away!' he promised. 'But if I've got to improvise spare parts—well . . .'

'Just do your best, Jim!' Bob told him. 'You're our main hope, you know. Frankly, unless we can get out some sort of signal, I don't see how they'll locate us!'

Eve reappeared. She was worried about the James girl.

'She's going to have drugs sooner or later!' she warned Bob. 'There's a limit to how long we can keep her under with sleeping pills!'

'Everyone else okay?' Bob asked anxiously. 'Mrs Carson?'

'The grey-haired nanny is looking after her,' Eve told him. 'Goes by the name of Edith Hurst. She's a trained nurse so I've left Mrs Carson in her hands. Mrs Carson doesn't look too good, I'm afraid. I hope there's no internal injury.'

'And the other passengers?'

'The old couple were a bit shaken but they're better after a cup of tea. Apart from the fact that he broke his glasses, they're okay now.'

John returned with Bruce Mallory to report that the three Nigerians were now safely, if none too comfortably, secured in the hold. They'd stripped them down to their underwear so knew they didn't have any other weapons.

'The fight's gone out of them!' Bruce said with satisfaction. 'These thugs are all the same —disarm them and they're nothing.'

'There's a girl back there making an awful fuss because she wants her luggage!' John said grinning. 'Uppity piece, too. A deb, shouldn't wonder. I told her she'd just have to wait a while!'

'I'd forgotten all about her,' Bob said grinning. 'She must be the eloping heiress! Eve said her picture was in the *Express* this morning! Wonder if she's right!'

'The young man with her didn't look like a pop singer to me!' Bruce said wryly. 'Hair's as short as mine!'

'Who cares anyway!' John broke in. 'We've enough to worry about without them. Are we going to get the luggage out?'

'Not tonight!' Bob said. In the last few minutes it had quite suddenly got dark. He sent John off to switch on the lights. The grey gloom inside the passengers' cabin wasn't going to make any of them feel very cheerful about their predicament. No doubt with the same thought in mind, Mary-Lou had switched on the taped music. The passengers who had been watching the sunset were becoming restless. The fascination of the desert sunset had given way to delayed fear. Only now were people realising that they were alone in the hostile environment of the great Sahara; that civilisation was a long way off.

Eve and Mary-Lou began to prepare supper trays. The food they had taken on board when they refuelled at Rome airport now acquired a new meaning. This and the few edibles they carried permanently would be all that stood between the thirty-nine people on board and starvation. The girls were uncertain just how much they should hand out tonight. Too little and the passengers might realise they could be in far greater danger than they had so far appreciated; too much and the comparatively meagre stocks might run out long before the search planes located them.

It was Bruce Mallory who settled the

argument for them. Appearing in the door of the galley, he smiled at Eve and said:

'If you'll forgive the interference, ladies, my boss has asked me to inform you that as head of the passengers' committee, formed as of ten minutes ago, food is to be strictly rationed. He suggests nothing more than cheese and biscuits and lots of hot coffee; half rations for the prisoners. And as soon as you girls have a moment, I'm to ask you for a detailed list of every calory we have on board and the duration of time you expect the various items to remain in edible condition. Okay?'

They nodded. Mary-Lou said tentatively:

'How long does Bob expect we'll be here— before we're rescued, I mean? You make it sound as if it could be a long time.'

Bruce mustered a smile, caught Eve's eye and said reassuringly:

'As far as I could gather, we *could* be found tomorrow. The rationing is just a precaution in case it turns out to be a day or two longer than he believes likely. After all, if we go carefully we could last for weeks if we had to, though personally I doubt we'll be here that long!'

Eve gave him a grateful smile. She herself thought it quite possible that they could be lost here for a very long time. She knew Bob hadn't been able to send out signals. The Sahara was a mighty big place to search, not to mention the fact that they'd possibly be scouring the Mediterranean and not the desert for the lost V.C.10.

She followed Bruce out of the galley and into a quiet corner of the cabin.

'Thanks for sounding so cheerful to Mary-Lou, but you don't have to put on an act for me,' she said quietly. 'I'm aware of the spot we're in. The truth is we might never be found. Not a very happy thought!'

The American looked down at Eve's serious face and decided that this girl could be relied on not to panic. He felt curiously elated by the knowledge that she could face the possibility of death without going to pieces. She was the kind of woman he could respect and he wanted to be able to respect her.

He put a hand over hers.

'We'll make the best of it, whatever Fate has in store for us. I don't *want* to die and guess I don't really believe we are going to die, but if it should happen—well, I suppose it sounds crazy but I'm glad *you'll* be around.'

'Which is more than I am!' Eve said with an attempt at humour to cover her sudden embarrassment.

This man had the strangest effect upon her. He made her aware not only of himself but of herself, as a woman. It was as if he had an extra sense and could see into her mind. It unnerved her to think he might have guessed she wasn't anything like as unaffected by his presence as she pretended. It was far too soon to be close to someone else. First she wanted to get to know him; to find out if she really did like, respect, trust him. Yet he had a way of side-stepping all these preliminaries and establishing a relationship that made it seem as if they had known each other for years.

He was silent now, standing quietly beside her but so close that their arms touched. Eve felt the first tremor of physical attraction; found herself wondering whether he, too, was conscious of the contact and affected by it as she was. She wanted to move away yet remained perfectly still.

'So long as I stay here, with him, I'm safe!' she thought irrationally.

The passengers were beginning to make preparations for the night. Some were fixing up make-shift beds with the blankets and pillows which had been distributed in the forward half of the cabin. Mary-Lou was taking round the first of the supper trays to those who had returned to their seats.

'I must go and help,' Eve murmured. 'She must be tired.'

'You, too!' said Bruce, moving away and so releasing her from the invisible bond which had held her to him. 'Later this evening I'll work out a job schedule so some of the passengers can help. Those three girls would be of use, I'm sure.'

He nodded towards the three young hairdressers who were already doing their best to be of assistance by carrying blankets and pillows forward for the two old-age pensioners. Then he looked back at Eve, his eyes holding hers in a question.

'Perhaps we'll have a chance to talk later? There's so much we have to talk about. Agreed?'

Eve nodded. There wasn't time, in these circumstances, for pretence. In the ordinary way, she would have played a little more 'hard to get', but she, too, wanted to talk; to find out more about him. For all she knew he could be married. She hoped not. She'd had enough of married men . . .

She gave herself a mental shake. This was no time for such thoughts. She went back to the galley to join Mary-Lou. But even whilst her fingers deftly laid out food on the trays obedient to her will, her mind continued to play truant. If Bruce Mallory were married she wasn't going to get involved. It wasn't as if the friendship mattered at this stage; he couldn't possibly mean anything to her any more than she could mean anything to him.

But her emotions rejected this logic. Somewhere, in Bruce's face, in his eyes, the touch of his arm, he had made her aware that there *was* something between them; something more than mere physical attraction, though that existed, indisputably.

With a great effort, Eve forced herself to put the thought of Bruce Mallory to the back of her mind as she busied herself making the hot coffee all of them needed. There was still a lot to be done before she could relax. Later, she would try to think out coolly and logically what was happening to her and why a man—any man—could be of the slightest importance when it was more than probable that a slow and agonising death lay only days away.

The fact was, she thought, that if she were going to die, then so be it—but first, while there was still time, she wanted really to live.

CHAPTER FIVE

Edith Hurst helped Leanora Carson back into her seat. Her new employer looked very ill.

'Are you sure there's nothing I can do, Mrs Carson?'

With an effort, Leanora brought herself back from the black mists of pain in which she seemed to be engulfed. She tried to smile.

'I'm very much afraid, Nanny, that the jolt I took when we landed . . .' she paused to gasp as a new wave of pain shot through her abdomen . . . 'I think I may be miscarrying.'

Only her years of training prevented Edith Hurst from showing her real feelings of dismay. An aeroplane, grounded in the Sahara with no doctor or medical advice available, was hardly the place to have a miscarriage. But she said soothingly:

'Well, if that's the case, dear, I'd better see that nice young American and see if we can get you some privacy.'

Leanora looked up with a grateful smile.

'I'm glad . . . you're here,' she whispered. 'I'm so sorry!'

It flashed across Edith Hurst's mind that she, too, was likely to be sorry if Mrs Carson really were to lose her baby. It was typical of the way Fate had dictated her life . . . always just missing out at the eleventh hour. There was her intended marriage to Ted so many years ago now she seldom thought about it any more—he'd been killed in a train accident a week before their wedding.

Next to come on the list of thwarted ambitions was her desire to become a nurse. She'd felt she could face life without Ted if she could devote herself to the sick. It would have been a compensation. But a year short of her qualifying exams, her mother had contracted cancer and at the end of a long, slow, painful death, had left Edith alone in the world and penniless. There'd been no money even to pay for the funeral. Edith had had to borrow from a distant relative.

So at the age of twenty-five, she had taken her first job as a nanny. It lasted only a few years and had been succeeded by another which had promised permanency. But that, too, had come to an abrupt and unexpected end when the husband, who was a television producer, suddenly lost his job and the family could no longer afford a nanny for the three children to whom she had become devoted.

Edith took stock of her situation and decided she was of an age and now had enough experience to realise at least one of her ambitions in life—to travel and see the world. She answered an advertisement put in *The Times* by an American couple who were promising to continue employment in the United States after their stay in England terminated. But they had failed to keep their promise. War had been declared and her employers rushed back to safety in their own country without stopping to make the necessary arrangements for visas and permits to take Edith with them.

Edith went to work in a factory, making munitions. An American airman fell in love with her—or so she had believed—and asked her to marry him when he came back from Italy where he was to become part of the occupation forces. She did not find out until the war was over that he was already married. He wrote from America telling her he was sorry he'd lied to her; that he really had been fond of her but had returned to his wife.

Edith gave up any further thought of marriage. She settled back into life as a nanny once more. The years passed and the children grew up and went off to their boarding schools. Edith stayed on as 'mother's help'.

Her employers were feeling the results of the financial depression that had settled over post-war England. She was now in her fifties and dreaded a change although deep down in her heart she knew it was inevitable. She voluntarily took lower and lower wages but six months ago, she had finally been told she must leave.

Commonsense told her that her employer was right when she said it was in Edith's best interests that she leave before she was too old to get another job. Now, with her wonderful references, she would still be able to make a fresh start.

The heart had gone out of her. For three months she had sat at home—a bedsitter in a cheap part of Surbiton, and fretted. Then she had seen Leanora Carson's advertisement in the *Telegraph*. At first she had only toyed with the idea of applying for the post, thought about it in terms of 'wouldn't it have been just the very thing I wanted in the old days'. Then, slowly, it had begun to seem possible. The advertisement had said: *Mature* . . . If they weren't looking for a *young* nanny, she might stand a chance . . . Cairo . . . the Middle East . . . abroad . . . and a new baby due . . .

Edith trod firmly on the familiar temptation for self-pity. This was not the time to be sorry for herself. Poor Mrs Carson . . . she must do what she could to help.

Bruce Mallory looked at the thin, grey-haired woman aghast.

'But she can't have a miscarriage . . . not now!' he said.

Despite herself, Edith smiled.

'I'm afraid we can't prevent it, Mr Mallory,' she said dryly.

Bruce grimaced.

'Well, we'll just have to do what we can. Tell me what you want and I'll try and organise it.'

With remarkable efficiency, it was only a short while before he had rigged up a curtained-off apartment in the forward cabin. With ingenuity and Eve's help, he fixed up poles and used the curtains dividing the galley from the passengers' cabin. At Edith's suggestion he improvised a 'bed' by forcing down the backs of two seats. Eve went round the passengers asking those who could to produce towels and other requisites Edith had said might be needed. Leanora Carson was undressed, put into a borrowed nightie and into bed.

She lay, in comparative comfort now, fighting the pain. She thought about Granville and Paul, and she thought about Peter. She thought about God and wondered if this was His hand at work. Did He mean her to be free of the child so that she could go back to Peter?

If only she could believe that! But in her heart she knew it couldn't be so. She'd never been free to go to Peter—not since the day she'd married Granville.

She thought then about death . . . and knew that she didn't care if she died. It would be a relief from all the miserable torture of living not to have to worry any more about anything or anyone. Paul wouldn't really miss her; Granville would be shocked, but not really *hurt*. And Peter? He must already have accepted the fact that she was 'dead' to him anyway. In a way, when time healed the pain, he would be happier, too, for he'd know the futility of loving a ghost.

She slept a little. Edith had given her a pill—she wasn't sure what—but it had deadened the pain and helped her to doze. She lost count of time. Whenever her eyes opened, Edith was there beside her. She was grateful—deeply so. It would be someone's hand to hold as the pain got worse. And she knew it would.

*   *   *

'Are you scared?' Ann whispered in the darkness.

The three girls had settled down for the night. They were reasonably comfortable and warm beneath the blankets.

'A bit!' Denise whispered back. 'It's the not knowing *when* we'll be rescued, isn't it?'

Janet listened to their voices in the darkness and knew that she, too, was afraid. The others might talk of rescue but as far as she could work it out, there was no guarantee they would be found. If the radios were not functioning and no one in the whole world knew where they were . . .

She turned her thoughts quickly away from such fears. Her eyes found the tiny glimmer of light up in the forward cabin. She knew that must be where the poor woman was having a miscarriage. She knew, too, by the look on his face when he didn't think anyone was watching him, that the American was worried. He kept a cheerful smile on for the passengers but Janet had heard him telling the blonde stewardess that it was 'going to be a bit tricky'. She wondered if the woman would die. Did people die of miscarriages? If only there were a doctor on board!

Her thoughts wandered back to England and home. She hoped her parents did not know yet that the plane was overdue at Cairo. How frantic they would be, her father especially, for he'd always adored her. He'd been the one to encourage her whenever she was doubtful about trying anything new. Even this trip . . . he had been the one to say: 'It'll be a fine adventure!' Mum hadn't wanted her to go but Dad had talked her round. Would he blame himself if . . . until he knew they were safe and sound?

Janet sighed. Whatever happened tomorrow, she was not going to let anyone see she was afraid. She'd stay outwardly cheerful and see that the other two girls were, too. They were younger than she . . . she must set them an example.

'Bet the boys will be worried about us!' she said to divert them. 'We'll certainly have something exciting to tell them when we get back!'

'If we get back!' Ann said tremulously.

'Oh, go on with you, Ann!' Janet chided her. 'You know very well it's only a matter of time—and we've lots of food and water to last for weeks. I heard the red-headed American say so.'

Denise suddenly came into the conversation, her voice sounding considerably more normal.

'I must be going mad, Jan!' she said. 'I clean forgot to tell you . . . when I went up front to wash, that dark-haired pilot spoke to me—not the Captain—the other one. Wanted to know my name and where we three were going and how we were making out. Seemed really interested, too.'

'Watch it!' Ann said giggling. 'Denise is on the make!'

'Alas and alack but Denise isn't!' said the younger girl. 'It wasn't me he was interested in but you, Jan. He asked me, quote: "Who's the pretty girl with the reddish-blonde hair?"'

Janet found she was holding her breath. She knew very well to whom Denise was referring—not one of the pilots but the radio operator, Jimmy Tate. Twice they had passed one another in the aisle, not speaking but on each occasion he had given her the nicest smile! So he thought she was pretty and had wanted to know her name. It was a pleasant thought. She had been curious enough about him to ask the younger of the stewardesses what *his* name was!

'You seem to forget I'm practically engaged to Allan,' she chided her two friends, but it was she who had forgotten Allan. She was quite shocked to realise that she hadn't given him a thought since she'd kissed him goodbye at the airport.

'Do I really love him?' she asked herself now. She and Allan had known each other since school days and they'd more or less drifted into going steady. It hadn't been a sudden fantastic falling in love the way you read about in books. It had been something which had happened almost without her knowing it. She was very fond of him and he of her. Their going together had been a natural thing and everyone just assumed it would stay that way. Mum and Dad had often asked her when she and Allan were going to take the plunge. But there hadn't seemed any hurry and although Allan sometimes spoke about the future in terms which obviously included her, he'd never actually said: 'Will you marry me?' He'd taken it for granted, the way she had, that one day they would.

It seemed awful that she could really have

forgotten his very existence. She'd wanted Allan to come on this trip and had only given way when she realised that if Allan went, it would more or less force Denise's and Ann's boy friends to be included in the invitation and the girls were adamant that they wanted to go unattached. Mum had said she thought it wouldn't be such a bad thing if she and Allan didn't see each other for a few weeks. 'Jolly him up a bit!' was Mum's comment and she'd been right—when Allan heard they were going off for a whole month without him, he'd finally started talking about getting engaged. Janet, who'd waited a long time for him to ask her, suddenly found herself resentful because he hadn't done so ages ago! She realised that he'd taken her completely for granted for years and years and her vanity was sufficiently piqued to make her vague about the engagement. 'Perhaps, when I get back!' she'd said, knowing very well that she would say yes!

Now, suddenly, she wasn't so sure. If she could be attracted to a young man who was little more than a complete stranger to her, was she really ready for marriage to Allan? If she really loved him, would she be feeling so pleased because Denise said Jimmy Tate called her pretty? Or was she just being stupidly romantic? With the plane crash and being marooned in the Sahara and everything, life had become a bit unreal—more like a film she was watching and she could be casting herself in the role of heroine with Jimmy Tate as the hero! She was a romantic, though she took care to hide the fact from anyone else for fear they would think her 'soft'. Most of the girls she knew seemed to take life so casually—drifting in and out of affairs and not, in Janet's view, really being in love at all. It was all sex. Allan was a bit that way, too . . . always had sex on the brain and spent half their time together trying to talk her into sleeping with him. Or he used to—before he'd given it up as a bad job. He often accused her of being cold but she wasn't really—not inside. It was partly because she knew herself capable of violent passion that she felt it necessary to exert an iron control upon herself—and over Allan. Once started, she wouldn't be able to treat sex casually, she felt sure. But control over her actions did not prevent her imagination running riot, any more than she could prevent herself now wondering what it would be like to have Jimmy Tate make love to her.

Slightly ashamed of her thoughts, she diverted her two friends' attention away from the subject of boys and pretended not to notice when Jimmy passed down the aisle and wished her a very good night!

*　　　*　　　*

It was nearly midnight when the last of the

passengers finally settled down to sleep. Eve had been assisting Edith Hurst with that poor woman, Leanora Carson. The experience had exhausted her. Apart from the pain Mrs Carson suffered, Eve had found herself deeply affected by the personal tragedy which had become all too apparent as the hours went by and Mrs Carson's condition, weakened by suffering, brought her to a state of semi-consciousness. She began to whisper the name of a man called Peter. Again and again she called for him, tears pouring down her cheeks as fast as Eve could wipe them away. Eve knew very well from the name on the passenger list that this was not Mrs Carson's husband. His name was Granville. There was such urgency, such an agony of longing in her tone of voice that Eve had been forced to realise this Peter could only be a lover. She wondered if the nanny, so calm and silent, had reached the same conclusion. If so, she gave no sign but administered to Mrs Carson's needs as best she could.

Strange, thought Eve, as she climbed down out of the aircraft into the cold moonlit isolation of the desert, how someone else's sufferings, mental and physical, had such power to affect her. She had thought, after her own private agony, that she was beyond caring how others felt! Instead, it had somehow made her more conscious of the depth of a woman's suffering when she was parted from the man she loved. She found herself wondering about this mythical 'Peter'. Was it his child that the woman had miscarried? Was she going to him or away from him? Would he be waiting to reassure and comfort her? To give her another child? They were questions to which she would probably never know the answers.

She shivered. After the intense heat of the day and the warmth inside the plane, the night air was cutting in its sharp coldness. Yet how beautiful the desert looked in the brilliant moonlight. How vast and empty and desolate it appeared. Loneliness and fear caught at her throat and the tensions of the whole dramatic day suddenly engulfed her. The shivering increased until she could not control it.

Suddenly, she felt two warm strong arms enfold her from behind her back. She felt herself being gently turned round and found herself standing face to face with Bruce Mallory. He did not speak but drew her slowly against him until their bodies were locked against each other in a fierce, almost frantic embrace.

Eve made no attempt to release herself. The feel of firm, male arms about her, his strange masculine smell, were so completely what she needed in this moment of weakness, that she clung to him openly and desperately. If she were to die, then she thanked God that here was a man who wanted to hold her in his arms and make death that much easier. She would be less afraid here, within his embrace, than if she were alone. If she had to die, then at least she would have these few days in which to live fully once again. Woman without man was never complete and she had been far, far too long alone.

But she said nothing and he remained silent, holding her until the shivering of fear gave way to a different kind of trembling. Then he kissed her. A thousand thoughts whirled madly through Eve's brain as his mouth searched for hers. He was a stranger. What must he be thinking of her? She didn't even know him. This was crazy, impossible. But soon feeling transcended thought and she made no protest when he began to walk her away from the plane to a deeply shadowed indentation in the sand a hundred yards behind its great grey body.

She had not noticed before but he had a blanket draped across his shoulders. As they reached the sandy hollow he laid it down and kneeling there, gently pulled her down after him. She sensed the sudden change of his mood. The urgency had gone and now he was quiet, tender, almost compassionate as he knelt facing her, his two hands raised to cup her face.

For the first time, he spoke. 'You are not afraid, Eve?' His voice, with its barely perceptible American accent, moved her strangely. She shook her head. She felt many emotions, but not fear.

He traced the line of her eyebrows and then his fingers, cool and gentle, caressed her cheek and outlined her lips.

'You are very beautiful!' he said. 'I had forgotten a woman could be so lovely!'

She was surprised. She would have imagined that this man would have attracted many women; that no matter what else in his life might be barren, it would not be his sex life. Yet he spoke as if he had not known a woman for a long time.

His next words surprised her further.

'You're not married, are you?' he said, and when she shook her head, added: 'Nor am I, though I was once. I haven't wanted a woman since—until now. I want you, Eve. Does that offend you?'

Curiously, it did not. She had felt his desire and honesty forbade pretence. If he could be honest, so could she.

'I was alone just now, before you came,' she said in a low voice although they were too far from the plane for anyone to have heard them. 'I was realising for the first time that . . . that we might all die. I was suddenly very frightened. Now it doesn't seem so terrifying. I'm not frightened now. But I don't want to die. I want to live . . .'

'I know! You may think this uncomplimentary but it sure isn't meant that way. I want to tell you that the way I feel—it isn't just from fear of death and a contrary wish to grab the last remnants of life that might be left. It's more than that. I was attracted by you before ever I knew the plane was in trouble. What subsequently happened—well, it only served to make me feel even more certain that you were my kind of woman. You were so cool and calm and yet all the time so feminine . . . I wanted you then. What has happened isn't the reason for the way I feel—only the reason I'm saying all this now—because there might not be time to say it next week or next month or next year. Do you understand? Had we not been in any danger, I would have waited.'

Eve nodded. She understood him perfectly. His words somehow made everything all right and never once did she doubt his sincerity. In the darkness she smiled.

'If there had been time, I expect I would have made the effort to play "hard to get",' she said. 'Perhaps we should be glad we can take this short cut.'

Somewhere at the back of her mind, Eve felt that sanity must ultimately return; that tomorrow she might have regrets; that if they all got out of this mess and life returned to normal, she would remember this night as an improbable dream. But for the moment nothing seemed surprising until they lay side by side in the moonlight and he said:

'If we ever come out of this alive, Eve, if things work out—do you think you could love me?'

'I don't know . . .' she said hesitantly. 'I didn't know I could feel like this—so close, I mean—and we're really strangers. I was in love once—at least I thought I was.'

As she spoke she felt a sudden deep revulsion of self. She wished there had never been another man in her life; that this was the first time she had felt so dangerously attracted by any man; that she could have told him it was the first time.

'You look sad, darling. Tell me?'

He used the endearment quite naturally. His arms were round her holding her close, and suddenly, it was easy to talk. By nature reserved, she had not been able to confide in a girl friend or parent, the sufferings of that past unhappy affair. It had remained bottled up within her, retaining its power to distress her; filling her so often with bitterness and cynicism. Somehow Bruce Mallory had wiped the slate clean. The past had ceased to hurt . . . and she could tell him about it.

He held her close whilst the words came pouring out. Only once did he interrupt to say 'My poor baby!' When she finally reached a faltering conclusion, he kissed her with surprising tenderness.

'Don't regret it, Eve!' he told her. 'Think of it, if you must remember, as an experience from which you learned something, even if it was a hard lesson to learn. It doesn't do to waste your life in regrets. I, too, have done just that, only for different reasons.'

He told her briefly about his marriage and how he had rejected any deep emotional involvement since in order to avoid being hurt a second time.

'You've made me realise the folly of it!' he said, smiling. 'Now I'm alive again and I thank God for it, and you, Eve.'

They talked far into the night. Once Eve left to go back to the plane to make sure she was not needed. Nearly everyone was asleep with the exception of Mrs Carson and the nanny, and the parents of the girl who was still under sedation. Eve went into the little galley and made coffee which she carried back into the darkness to Bruce, together with another blanket for they had begun to feel the extreme cold.

As dawn began to break they lay closely entwined, watching the incredible miracle of a desert sunrise. As the colours changed from eggshell blue to primrose yellow and daffodil gold, Bruce said:

'To have experienced this, with you beside me, will make anything and everything that is to come worth while. Wrong though I may be even to think so, I am not sorry we've been forced to land here. I feel horribly guilty about it, but I'm glad!'

She smiled back at him.

'I feel it, too, though maybe both of us will

109

change our minds if things get tough. Oh, Bruce, I don't want to die now. I want to live . . . I want to go on knowing you; to find out everything there is to discover about you. I know so little. You're still almost a stranger!'

But both knew that they had passed this stage long ago, before the dawn. There was a tangible close intimacy between them now which defied all conventional barriers. The externals of their lives did not matter and they were already three parts of the whole way in love.

It was Bruce who insisted they return to the plane before it grew any lighter. Already the first half of the sun had crossed the horizon and the warmth was beginning to steal back into the air.

'I've got to think of your reputation even if you won't!' he told her. 'A lot of people might think we'd been making love. Perhaps we have, in a way, but not that way and I won't have your good name in jeopardy. Besides, you're going to have a tough day ahead of you, darling. You must get some sleep!'

He kissed her once more at the door of the plane. His eyes were laughing and tender both at once.

'I'm going to have a difficult job keeping away from you in there!' he said, nodding towards the cabin. 'Everyone who sees my face when I look at you is bound to guess how I feel about you!'

'I don't care. Do you?' Eve laughed back.

Sheer exhaustion helped her to achieve two hours of deep refreshing sleep before Mary-Lou touched her shoulder and whispered that some of the passengers were already awake and she thought they should take round tea. If she had noticed Eve's absence in the night she did not refer to it. Eve was grateful. Part of her wished to talk about Bruce and about nothing else but Bruce; yet part of her wanted to hug her secret close to her heart, sharing the knowledge of her wakening love with no one else but him.

CHAPTER SIX

Leanora Carson was very ill. Edith Hurst reported to Bob at dawn that if medical help were not soon forthcoming, her employer would almost certainly die.

'Haven't we anything on board that will help?' Bob asked, aghast at this news.

'I'm afraid she's haemorrhaging badly, Captain. She ought to have a transfusion. She's very weak.'

'And you couldn't give a blood transfusion?' Bob asked, knowing even as he spoke that this wouldn't be possible. Although Edith Hurst had nursing experience, she couldn't possibly know about blood groups and even if the passengers volunteered blood, they had not the facilities for testing the groups.

He drew a deep sigh, partly of anxiety, partly of weariness. He'd slept only intermittently and the delayed shock of yesterday's events was taking its toll. Jimmy had worked all night, but without the spare parts necessary, he'd had to report failure to repair the radio. There was no hope now of making contact with the outside world. Their rescue from this disaster lay entirely in the hands of the search planes. They were not on any air route and with literally thousands upon thousands of square miles of uninhabited desert to be scoured, their chances of rescue were horribly remote.

Perhaps Leanora Carson's death, if such were to happen, would be the kindest death of all. For the rest of them it could well mean an agonisingly slow end from hunger and even worse, thirst. One of his first jobs this morning must be to put a very severe rationing on the water . . . but to do so would be to admit to the passengers the danger they were in. He didn't want a panic on his hands and yet even this would be preferable to undermining their chances of survival. As soon as he could, he intended to gather together a few of the more responsible passengers and form a committee to debate the whole ugly situation.

Meanwhile, there was Leanora Carson to be thought about. And there was also the young girl addict who was without the necessary drug to prevent her suffering the terrible symptoms of withdrawal. He had read about such things and knew that in very severe cases, it could be fatal. Was he going to have to face two deaths so soon?

At least John Wilson's report that the prisoners were still secure in the luggage hold was a relief although he was beginning to feel hourly less merciful towards them. He should have shot the three who were responsible for this mess. It would have meant that much more food and water for the rest of them. Maybe they should shoot them, he told himself wryly. They would certainly be given reduced rations for a start!

Eve and Mary-Lou, with the help of the three young hairdressers, served breakfast—coffee and a roll only. Bob took the opportunity to advise the more responsible of the passengers that he wanted them to form a committee—Kennedy Maxwell, Bruce Mallory, Edith Hurst and the crew. As soon as they had finished eating, they forgathered outside the plane.

The sun was already mounting in the sky. The temperature was climbing rapidly and would, Bob knew, soon soar over the 100°F. mark. It would be necessary for everyone to leave the plane soon, for its metal surface would attract the sun and it would become like an oven.

Briefly and factually he told the group of

people standing round him that, as he saw it, the position they were in was extremely grim—not entirely hopeless but certainly very forbidding. He asked for any ideas or suggestions that might help and told them he felt it was in everyone's best interests if the remainder of the passengers were put fully in the picture. Without the true facts, he did not feel he could expect their full co-operation over rationing and the strict adherence to the rules he believed they should draw up for everyone's safety.

As he had supposed, they took this opening statement calmly, as if they had all reached the same conclusion already. Suggestions were soon forthcoming. The luggage would be unloaded before it became too hot to work. Bruce offered to supervise this after nominating a small work party of the younger, fitter passengers to undertake the heavier physical tasks. Any food, drugs or medicines carried by any of the passengers would be handed in to Eve for the general good of the party. Edith Hurst, together with Eve, would supervise the issue of medicines and try to work out a diet on which they could survive as long as possible.

Kennedy Maxwell volunteered to act as a kind of personnel manager. With his background of diplomacy he felt he might be best suited to dealing direct with the passengers and their various problems. He would liaise with Bob on the administration of the rules. Whatever happened, they must keep law and order and Bob himself would act as the law in the event of infringements or disputes arising.

Mary-Lou, with the three girls, would undertake the domestic running of affairs. She would draw up a rota for jobs which could include the young newly wed Barlows, and the couple they now believed to be the teenage dopers. The football team would be useful members of Bruce's working party.

It now remained only for Bob to relay these facts and decisions to the passengers. With his newly formed 'committee' standing behind him, he spoke to the rows of upturned faces with as much firmness and confidence as he could muster.

'We'll get out of this sooner or later,' he said finally, 'if you will all co-operate, as I know you will. I don't like having to frighten you with possible dangers but unless we do face the facts now, we are not going to be able to last out if it should be "later" rather than "sooner". As soon as we have done a stocktaking of supplies, I'll be able to give you a better idea of how long we can stick it out. Meanwhile, let's all get down to work to make ourselves more comfortable. We'll rig up a tent outside where it will be considerably cooler during the day. For the sake of hygiene, we'll build two more latrines some distance from the plane.

We will also rig up petrol flares so that we can signal any plane that comes looking for us. Now one last thing—time is likely to hang a bit heavy and I'd be glad if anyone has cards or games of any sort if they would hand them over to Mr Maxwell here, who will do his best to see that they benefit the maximum number of people. Thanks for listening and for taking this so well.'

There was no panic. Only Mr and Mrs James, parents of the sick girl, looked completely devastated by the news. Anticipating this, Eve was standing near them and tried to soothe them. The girl was becoming restless and Eve herself felt some of the parents' apprehension.

The plane became a hive of movement. In a surprisingly short time, the luggage was spread around on the sandy floor of the desert and contents were being brought to a table which had been roughly erected in the newly built 'tents' beneath the shade afforded by the V.C.10's great wings. Some passengers were even smiling as they came up with their private possessions and handed them in to Eve.

'It's only a packet of Disprins but . . .'

'I was taking these chocolates to my aunt in Natal . . .'

'Would T.C.P. be any use? I always carry a spare bottle . . .'

Supplies mounted. To Eve's surprise, the young girl, Sarah, had volunteered her assistance and was now neatly sorting out food from medicines. She seemed almost to be enjoying the situation.

'Well, it all helps to pass the time!' Sarah said languidly. 'I suppose it has got a funny side, too—I mean, when I stop to think I am only on this plane by a sheer fluke . . .'

In a short burst of confidence, she told Eve the facts.

'I suppose you think I'm mad!' she said at last. 'I'm beginning to think so myself so you don't have to be afraid to agree with me.'

'And you really love him—this Larry Bell?'

Sarah's pretty face screwed up into a childish grimace.

'I thought I did. Maybe I don't. I think it was mainly to spite Father. One gets so fed up being told what you can and what you can't do. My parents are so prejudiced—that's what I can't stand. I mean, they'd damn Larry for nothing more than class—as if that mattered these days!'

'You're very young to think of settling down for life with one person,' Eve said slowly. 'One can be so wrong when one is young. I know—I once thought I was madly in love and now I know . . .'

'Well, there's always divorce,' Sarah broke in impatiently. 'Anyway, I probably won't be able to marry him now. If we get out of this mess, Father will have a whole posse of people waiting for us at the other end. I just hope I

117

can talk him out of having Larry clapped into gaol.'

Later, Larry himself approached Eve. He gave her a grin she found rather disarming.

'That crazy bird of mine says she's told you the whole story!' he said. 'So you know who I am and at least I can drop the guise of Henry Bard, thank God. I guess it was a rotten idea from the start. Now, if we do get rescued, I'll face a conviction for seducing a minor or something. Not a soul in hell will believe it was all *her* idea!'

'I believe it!' Eve said smiling. 'So keep your chin up—if I do, others might!'

But he refused to be cheered up.

'It'll go against me,' he said bitterly. 'My background and all that. And then there's the drugs angle—that'll come out. Past convictions always do.'

Eve looked up frowning.

'You've been in prison for taking drugs?'

'No—fined—first offence. But I still take the stuff—soft drugs only, of course. They're bound to find traces in my flat.'

'You're not still on drugs?' Eve asked.

Larry shrugged.

'Well, I'm not sure what you mean by that. I'm not an addict but I use it when I need it. I always carry it around in case I want a buzz. I can take it or leave it.'

Eve grabbed his arm.

'Look, Larry, you might be able to help. It's

118

important. You know the sick girl—the one they've put in the second tent with Mrs Carson? She's an addict and she hasn't any supplies with her. What you take—would it help? She's very ill!'

'Depends what she's been taking. You can have my stuff if it's any good. Like me to see her? Maybe I can do something.'

But Eve was already on her feet and hurrying him over to talk to Kennedy Maxwell. Elsie and Harold Curry sat beneath the wing of the plane stitching blankets together to form a great curtain similar to the one now hanging from the other wing. Propped on the wing top with suitcases filled with sand to weigh them down, they formed an efficient barrier to the burning rays of the sun. Seats had been taken out of the plane and placed on the sand within the pool of shade for those who had time to sit. For the moment, everyone else was busy.

'Looks like they expect us to be here some time.' Harry spoke thoughtfully to his wife. 'Are you frightened, dear?'

Elsie managed a smile which hid the anxiety in her heart. She was very frightened but she did not intend to load that on to Harold who would then worry for her as well as for himself.

'It's quite an adventure, isn't it?' she said cheerfully. 'We'll have something to tell our Celia, won't we?'

Harold nodded, relieved that his wife could

be thinking in terms of a future when they would see and talk to Celia again. The way he saw it, this might never happen now. It was a heartbreaking thought when they'd spent so very long saving up to visit her. It had been Elsie's dearest wish just to see Celia once more. Now it might never happen.

He eased the shirt away from his neck. How hot it was getting! Some of the young men were already stripped to the waist. It was difficult to breathe in this heat, even in the comparative cool of the shade they sat in. He could see Elsie's dress damp between the shoulder blades and beneath her armpits and knew that she, too, must be feeling the heat though she didn't complain.

'Would you like a drink, dear?' he asked. 'I'm sure they'd give me something if I asked.'

But his wife shook her head quickly.

'I'm not all that thirsty,' she lied. 'Besides, dear, you know what the Captain said about the water supply. We must keep to our ration the same as everyone else.'

He nodded but privately made up his mind to watch Elsie. He knew his wife—she was the sort who'd go without her ration if someone else needed it more. In this heat it was important to replace the liquid the body lost in evaporation. He didn't intend to have his Elsie ill like that lady on the other side of the plane. Elsie had asked the nanny how she was and relayed to him the fact that Mrs Carson was very weak. It seemed the poor woman wouldn't put up any real fight for life, yet she had seemed to be a person of substance—wealthy, beautiful and still young. Perhaps this was one good thing about not having a radio contact with the outside world—at least her poor husband couldn't know how bad she was.

But Edith Hurst knew. She had little doubt now that it was only a matter of hours before her employer died. And Leanora Carson knew, too, for twice in her semi-coma she had asked Edith to fetch her a priest.

Edith went in search of Eve.

'There's nothing we can do for her physically,' she said quietly. 'But if we could ease her mind—she is very distressed. I'm a Roman Catholic myself so I understand her wish for absolution. Without it, one dies in sin, you understand?'

Eve shook her head wearily. Tiredness was beginning to tell upon her and she wasn't sure how she could continue to cope with all these seemingly insoluble problems people kept bringing to her. She would like to help poor Mrs Carson but . . .

'Anything I can do?'

Bruce Mallory's calm voice soothed the moment of hysteria instantly. She gave him a grateful smile.

'I don't see what we *can* do,' she said, explaining the position.

'If she could just make her confession . . .'

Edith put in tentatively, with a strange look at Bruce which Eve did not at first grasp. Then Bruce said quietly:

'You think I should pretend to be a priest?'

Edith bit her lip. It was a very long time since she had been a practising Catholic. Somehow, when life had gone so wrong, instead of letting her Church help her, she had turned away from religion. Working for Protestant families had not assisted in her return to the fold, yet she knew, without doubt, that no matter how lax a Catholic she had been, she would not be able to die in peace without making her confession. Would God, the Almighty, frown upon such a masquerade were Mr Mallory to impersonate a priest? He need not say he was ordained. His offer to hear Mrs Carson's confession would infer it and she, poor soul, was too far gone to question the fact. If it would help her to die in peace, surely it could not be so sinful a thing to do? Surely the Heavenly Father would understand that they had no priest and must do the best they could?

'It could be a sin,' she whispered, more to herself than to the man standing beside her. 'I just don't know, Mr Mallory. I only know she won't be at peace until she has confessed.'

Eve looked at Bruce's face, stern, thoughtful and yet filled with compassion.

'I'll go to her,' he said without hesitation. 'I believe in a compassionate God.'

Eve followed a pace or two behind him. She was not sure if she believed in God at all. Until now, she would have stated she was a firm agnostic. But last night seemed strangely to have altered her whole attitude to life. Whether it was God or merely the whims of Fate which had sent Bruce Mallory into her life she neither knew nor cared. *He* was kind and not just when it suited his book to be so. He could gain nothing from what he was about to do for Mrs Carson. If he were a religious man, he might even be committing a sin. Yet he never hesitated.

It seemed at first as if they might be too late. Leanora was lying with her eyes closed, her breath barely audible. The paper whiteness of her skin made it almost transparent. But as Eve knelt beside her, she saw the pale lips move. 'Peter? Peter?'

Eve bit her lip in sudden compassion. It was a cruel Fate which now denied a woman the comfort of the man she loved in her last moments of life.

Now Bruce was bending over her. Eve watched as he took one of the lifeless hands and held it gently within his two firm, living ones.

'I am here!' he said in a strong but quiet voice. 'Did you want to talk to me, Leanora Carson?'

The glazed eyes opened. Watching them, Eve was sure that for one brief moment, joy radiated in them and a faint smile touched the bloodless lips. It was as if Leanora Carson were seeing her Peter at last. Then, as the eyes searched Bruce's face, she whispered: 'Will you hear my confession, Father?'

Eve stood up and put her arm round Edith's shoulders in a totally unconscious gesture. Each was near to tears and as they moved away they forbore to speak. Their mutual silence as much as their nearness was a comfort to them.

Leanora was also finding comfort. The night and the hours since the dawn had been vague and hazy to her. Sometimes she had dreamed of Peter, sometimes of Granville and Paul. Between bouts of these strange wandering dreams she had been aware of little Edith Hurst bending over her, giving her sips of water or wiping her face and wrists. She wasn't sure when she had first become aware that she was dying. She did not mind. It was easy to die; so much harder to live if living meant existing in a world without Peter. Her need for him was the only need of which she was really conscious until death moved a step closer. Then she knew that she could not die in mortal sin. Absolution alone could give her the certainty of a life hereafter. But the priest did not come and she hung on to life, waiting.

Now, at last, he was bending over her, his dark eyes gentle and his face merciful as if already prepared to absolve her from her sins.

Now she could confess her love for Peter. She knew that in the eyes of God their relationship was sinful but she could never believe it in her heart.

'I loved him so much!' she whispered. 'We loved each other.'

'God is love!' Bruce said softly. 'He will understand and forgive you.'

Sometimes he could not catch Leanora's words, they were so faint. He understood enough to appreciate her simple tragedy— marriage to a man she did not love because she believed her Peter was going to marry someone else; a son who was too like her husband ever to be in true harmony with her; the few brief weeks of happiness in London when love had been finally consummated but too late to affect the new child already in her womb.

Tears ran down Leanora's cheeks as she told Bruce how she had made the last final effort to part from Peter. But even this she saw as a sin, for never, not even now, could she deny that she had gone on sinning in her mind; that had God permitted her to live through this, she would have gone back to Peter now she had lost Granville's child.

'Don't ask me to repent, for I cannot, Father!' she said.

Bruce turned his eyes away from the tormented face of the dying woman. If he could think what to say; what to do to help her.

But he was hopelessly unqualified. He had not prayed since his wife's death; had forgotten how to pray.

Suddenly, he caught sight of a small leather-bound prayer book lying on the blanket. He grasped it with a sense of miraculous gratitude. Swiftly he turned to the Psalms and from the recesses of his memory turned to Psalm 121.

Quietly, steadily, he began to read aloud:

'I will lift up mine eyes unto the hills; from whence cometh my help' . . .

The beautiful words calmed him, as surely they were calming the dying woman.

Her eyes closed as if in sleep but he could see a faint movement of her lips as if she were repeating the words after him.

. . . 'so that the sun shall not burn thee by day: neither the moon by night. The Lord shall preserve thee from all evil; yea, it is even He that shall keep thy soul. The Lord shall preserve thy going out, and thy coming in; from this time forth' . . .

'I think she is dead, Mr Mallory.'

Edith Hurst's voice at his elbow brought his words to a halt. The tiny, grey-haired woman was gently folding the inert hands as if in prayer. Then she turned to Bruce and with a curiously beautiful smile, she said:

'Thank you very much. She died in peace thanks to you.'

Stiffly, Bruce rose to his feet. The words he would have liked to speak were stuck in his throat.

'That was always one of my favourite psalms!' Edith Hurst continued, as if aware of his emotion and doing what she could to give him time to recover himself. Gently, she reached out and took the prayer book from him. 'I'm glad I had this with me,' she said matter-of-factly. 'I very nearly didn't pack it and at the last minute, I put it in. Will you tell the Captain about Mrs Carson, sir, or shall I?'

Bruce drew a deep breath. He knew that the time would come when he would want to think more deeply about this episode in his life, but not now. Now he must return to the practicalities of the present. The poor woman who had just died would have to be buried—perhaps this evening in the comparative cool after sunset. What a terrible place for a grave—out in the wild wastes of the Sahara Desert! Someone must make a cross . . . a coffin. There was much to see to.

Slowly he walked out of the shadow of the make-shift sick bay, nodding briefly to the man and woman who were sitting either side of their daughter. To his surprise, the man followed him out into the sunshine.

'My name is James,' he said, inclining a shiny, nearly bald head at Bruce. 'I wanted to say that my wife and I couldn't help but overhear just now—the psalm, I mean. We prayed with you. You see, we need help, too, for our daughter, Jennifer.'

127

Bruce bit his lip.

'I'm not a priest,' he said nervously. 'I was just . . .'

'Yes, I know, but the words helped all the same. We thought, my wife and I, that it might be a comfort to others, too, if we could perhaps have a short prayer each evening . . . perhaps the Captain . . . ?'

'Yes, of course; I'll suggest it!' Bruce broke in. An hour ago he would have felt inclined to ignore such a suggestion but now, having been so close to death, he thought differently. They might all die before long. Let those who could, derive comfort from prayer. He himself felt emotionally drained. Too much had happened to him too quickly. And he couldn't keep pace with disaster, love and religion all in one package. He had stagnated in a world of non-feeling for so long, the events of the past twenty-four hours seemed like an assault upon his nervous system.

'I need a drink!' he thought, as he made his way round the plane to where his boss was still sitting at his improvised 'table'. The sight of that tall, upright figure bent over papers as Bruce had seen him a thousand times previously was strangely reassuring. Kennedy might almost be lost in consideration of some important political issue. Bruce's face relaxed into a smile. One thing now—politics weren't important here in the Sahara. They might have been the motivation for their being here in the first place, but the moment the plane touched down in the desert, they had ceased to matter. It was fundamentals now—survival, of the body and, perhaps, of the mind?

'Ah, Bruce, I want you!' Kennedy called out as he approached. 'How much sugar would you think it advisable to give each person every day? There are thirty-eight of us and we reckon in pounds. We've got about . . .'

'Thirty-seven of us now, sir,' Bruce said. 'I'm afraid Mrs Carson just died.'

Kennedy made no comment. He had the ability to remain silent when others might have been moved to talk. He saw the signs of strain on Bruce's face and realised that for some reason, the passenger's death had been a shock to him. He motioned Bruce into the empty seat beside him and pushed across the silver hip flask of brandy he always carried on him.

Silently, Bruce took it from him and raised it to his lips.

CHAPTER SEVEN

Jennifer James died that night. It had proved impossible to keep the details from the passengers since all had been involved in a pre-dawn search for her. She had seemed so much better the evening of the first long day.

The drugs Larry had given her had brought about a miraculous change and to her parents' delight, she talked to them rationally and even managed to eat a little of the food Eve gave her. Shortly after, she had smiled at her parents and later she had begged them to forgive her for all the trouble she had caused them and thanked them for everything they had done and were trying to do for her.

Eve told Bruce that she would never cease to blame herself for not realising that the girl was really bidding her parents farewell—that it should have been perfectly obvious to her, Eve, that the child had made up her mind to end her ruined life even at this moment.

But she had allowed her mother to tuck her down for the night and had soon closed her eyes and appeared to sleep. Exhausted, Eve, too, had turned in early and it had taken several minutes of calling and shaking by Mr and Mrs James before they had succeeded in rousing her to inform her that Jennifer was missing. It was four a.m.

'She left to go out for a breath of fresh air,' Mrs James told Eve in a panic-stricken whisper. 'I wanted to go with her but she insisted she would only be gone a few minutes—that it wasn't worth the trouble for me to get myself dressed. She seemed so . . . so normal and promised me she wouldn't go far. Oh, Miss Cunningham, I'm terribly afraid. It was so cold in the night . . . she's so thin . . . ill

. . . My husband and I have been searching for the past ten minutes—she's disappeared . . .'

They found her as the first beautiful eggshell blue of dawn lightened the sky in the east. On Kennedy's orders, no one had been permitted to go out of sight of the plane. It was far too dangerous, he'd warned them; too easy to get lost in the darkness. But as dawn broke and the circle of searchers widened, it was only a short while before Larry came staggering back to the plane carrying Jennifer's body, his face white and shocked. Sarah was sobbing beside him.

Kennedy did his best to convince the parents that their girl's death had been nothing more than a dreadful accident. Most of the passengers accepted this as the truth but Eve, Bruce, Kennedy and the grief-stricken Mr and Mrs James all knew in their hearts that Jennifer had decided to end her life the only way she knew how.

Kennedy was worried. The fact of two deaths in two days was taking its toll on the morale of the passengers. Moreover, the first numbed shock of their plight had worn off and naturally enough, they were beginning to speculate amongst themselves as to the chances of rescue. He was afraid that it might not be long before they fully appreciated, as he did, that rescue might never come. He debated with Bruce and the rest of the crew possible ways of distracting them. He rejected the suggestion of keeping them employed in making the camp more elaborate. To give them the idea that this was going to become anything but a very temporary place to live might increase the general air of depression.

They decided to fall back on organised games. When, at last, as evening approached, the hot day began to cool off, the football team put on a six-a-side exhibition match. A whist drive was arranged for those not interested in sport. Spirits began to revive as fresh ideas were put forward for the following day—they could play deck quoits: skittles, using empty bottles and a tennis ball. When it grew dark, they went back into the plane and played 'Twenty Questions', pitting a team made up of passengers against a team made up from the crew.

As the third day came to an end, Bruce congratulated Kennedy on managing so quickly to revive morale.

'Trouble is, though, that any kind of physical activity means a drain on strength and on water supplies. I'm not sure which is the more important.'

Bruce remained silent, glad that the ultimate decision was not his to make. It was up to Bob Sinclair, as Captain of the plane, and Kennedy, as elected spokesman for the passengers, to weigh the odds.

But turning the problem over in his mind, sleep evaded him. He could not escape from the frightening thought that death might not be very far away, whatever decisions Kennedy or Sinclair reached—a few weeks at most if they were not located. He didn't want to die. He wanted to live as he'd never before wanted life. He wanted to live like any normal human being—with Eve. It was strange, he told himself, how their relationship had developed these last two days. He found himself wanting to do ordinary everyday things with her; take her shopping, watch her cook supper in an ordinary kitchen in an ordinary flat; take her out to lunch; go swimming, dancing, skiing. He wanted to make love to her; to wake up in the morning and find her there and watch her smile and see that tense, anxious look of worry leave her face for ever. In short, he was daily falling more deeply in love with her. Passionately he wanted to get out of this mess—to live.

He wondered if Eve was feeling the same way. Since that first night in the desert, they had not had time to spend many hours alone together. He wanted to explain his feelings to her but both of them had been preoccupied helping to implement Kennedy's plans for the passengers. Nevertheless, they had exchanged looks, smiles, touched each other's hands, and an hour ago when she and Mary-Lou had turned in for the night, she had lifted her face quite naturally, as a child might have done, for him to kiss. It was almost as if he could feel as

133

a tangible thing, the lovingness of that light touch of her lips against his. Yet, desiring it so much, he could have imagined it.

'I can bear anything provided she loves me,' he thought in self-amazement.

In the little galley, Eve and Mary-Lou lay whispering in the darkness. It was the younger girl, not Eve, who was reiterating Bruce's thoughts.

'I think that as long as John holds me in his arms when the time comes, I could bear dying,' she confided. 'But I couldn't alone. That poor Jennifer, Eve. I can't stop thinking about her all alone out there in the desert. It's horrible.'

'Don't think about it,' Eve said gently. 'Or if you must, consider what her future might have been. Imagine what it could have been like for her parents. Maybe it's all for the best this way though naturally they are grieving terribly now.'

'I feel guilty, worrying about myself,' Mary-Lou confessed. 'I try to feel sorry for them but in the end I can only think of me—of John and me and the life we've planned together and may never have. I don't want to die, Eve. I want to live so much, so very much.'

'Silly girl—of course you're going to live—all of us are!' Eve replied confidently.

But she did not believe it. She had seen the look in Bob's eyes and in Kennedy's, too. She knew that hope was dwindling. Like Mary-Lou, she fought desperately against the idea of death. Ironically, she wouldn't have cared much a few years ago—not when that hopeless love affair had drawn to its inevitable conclusion and she'd firmly believed she'd never fall in love again. Death had been a temptation in those days, a comforting thought at the very back of her mind that there was always this last way out of her despair if it became too intolerable.

She wondered now if most people, women especially, had passed through such a stage when love seemed gone for ever. It was different for men—for whom love was only a part of existence. Life seemed to have little value for women without the men they loved and yet how wrong it was to give in to such thoughts. No one could know what life had in store.

Even she had never imagined such a man as Bruce Mallory coming into her life in so fateful a way; or that she herself could have grown to love someone so deeply in so short a while. She had known him three days and yet because of him, death was a terrifying thought; a fact that she could not and would not allow herself to contemplate or even consider.

Three days! It was not a long time in which to get to know someone and yet with her heightened awareness of him, she realised that she knew him very well indeed—far better than she had known other people who had been part of her life for years. But then, busy though she had been, there had not passed one minute when she had not been conscious of Bruce, never far away, helping, advising, comforting, encouraging, sympathising. How gentle and kind he had been with poor Mr and Mrs James! How sincerely he had read that beautiful psalm 'I will lift up mine eyes . . .' And how thoughtful he had been with the poor old nanny who seemed so lost now that she had no Leanora Carson to occupy her. How clever he had been to think of asking her to take care of Mrs James as he had not the time.

And with her personally, always that warm, embracing smile when their eyes met; always that swift intimate touch of his hand when he passed by, as if to say 'I'm thinking about you, too'. Somehow, all these little things had swamped completely the other link between them—the strong physical attraction which in the beginning had brought them so close—could it really be only three days ago?

Love! Eve thought sleepily about this greatest of all emotions. Real love brought out the best in human beings. It was only when love was a parody of the real thing that it hurt and injured and tormented. Both she and Bruce had suffered in the past. It was perhaps as well that they had, for now they could judge more easily the real from the false.

Kennedy Maxwell was also pondering the fact of love. Now that he had time to think about himself and his own life, he could, in the darkness of the cabin, give way for a moment to the terrible anxiety he felt for Nancy. Close as they were, he could not delude himself that telepathy was strong enough for her to know, thousands of miles away, that he was still alive; still safe for the moment. He could imagine all too easily the sleepless night she would be having, wondering, tormenting herself with the fear that he might be dead. In her shoes he would have been just as desperate. If only he could have sent her a message. Years ago, in the early days of their marriage when business had separated them for a night or two, she would beg him before he left to think of her.

'At eleven o'clock, Max!' (She never called him Kennedy.) 'Exactly at eleven o'clock and I'll do the same. Somewhere, somehow our thoughts will meet and I'll know you are thinking of me.'

He'd never failed to keep this tryst, yet in his heart he had not been able to believe that thoughts could travel into the ether and meet as she so fondly and childishly supposed. If he could believe it now! If, after all, she were right and thoughts could be transmitted, then surely she must be able to feel now that he was alive and thinking of her!

But even if wishing could make it so, he was not sure he would choose to have it that way. Like Bruce Mallory, he had faced facts squarely and he knew that death might not be far off. If Nancy could be sure he was alive now, then so would she be sure when death came to him and the mere thought of her grief was more than he could stand. Death itself did not frighten him. He did not believe in a hereafter but in complete nothingness, a cessation of existence. Death, therefore, was not to be feared—only the method of dying.

But Nancy, religiously inclined, believed firmly in a Heaven where she would meet again all those she loved.

'I won't mind dying when my time comes,' she had once told him. 'Providing I go first. Then I will know it's only a matter of time before you come to me, Max.'

What she could not bear was the thought that he might go before her. And now it looked as if this was the way it was going to be.

No, he did not mind so much for himself— he had had a good life and a happy one. He did not want to die but he could face it with some degree of courage if it were not for Nancy.

Suddenly he hit on the idea of writing to her. Sooner or later, even if it meant years and years later, someone would find the plane and his letter and give it to Nancy. She would at least know then that he was thinking of her, loving her and his letter might be of some comfort. And if they were located and rescued, then he could burn it or maybe even give it to her to laugh about—the sentimental farewell of a dying husband. No, Nancy would not

laugh—she'd cry and he would have to wipe
her tears away and tell her not to be such a
fool, weeping over something that never
happened!

'Tomorrow!' he told himself. 'I'll write
tomorrow.' Now he was too tired, too
exhausted both mentally and physically, to
fight any longer against the overwhelming
need for sleep.

CHAPTER EIGHT

Larry Bell also lay awake. Beside him, Sarah
lay curled up like the child she was, breathing
easily and deeply. One slender white arm lay
outside the rough grey blanket, drooped
lifelessly like that of the dead girl when he'd
found her, lying on her side, cold, lifeless.

His mind sheered away from the memory of
Jennifer. But not for long. No matter how
much he might wish to think of other things, in
the end his thoughts came back to that
shocking discovery of the body. They must
have been about the same age—Sarah and
Jennifer—kids, really. And both about as silly
as girls of that age can be. Raw, innocent kids,
avid for kicks and ignorant of the dangers.

He felt slightly sick. Something deep down
inside him was revolting against life. Dirty,
rotten place, this world. And he'd not done

139

much to make it less rotten, less dirty. Been too busy trying to crawl out from under the stone of poverty where he'd begun. Money had been his goal—money and fame—and he hadn't cared too much whose toes he'd trodden on to get them. Life—well, that wasn't worth a row of pins without the necessary and he'd gone all out for it—and got it. Now, suddenly, life had a different meaning. Water, enough of it, meant life in this bloody desert. A radio which worked—that meant life. A doctor who would have known how to stop Mrs Carson's haemorrhage—that meant life. And medical care and drugs for the girl whose body he'd handed back to her parents as if she'd been a sack of coal.

'So what do I care whether she died or not!' he told himself just as he'd already told himself a hundred times. She meant nothing to him—nor her parents either. He didn't give a damn about any living soul—not even Sarah. So what was he doing here in this God-forsaken desert eloping with a kid who was barely out of her nappies?

It had all been a lark, nothing more—a way to spite her old man for suggesting he wasn't good enough for his precious daughter. And who cared if he wasn't good enough! What was 'good enough' anyway? What did the old boy want? One of the Beatles, for God's sake?

No! he thought bitterly. He'd wanted a 'decent young man'—someone with a load of principles and upper-class standards and a receding chin. Why, the kid would be better off with him, Larry, than with that!

But would she? Lots of his pals took drugs—thought nothing of it. But Sarah . . . maybe if she once started, she'd be the kind who couldn't give it up—like that Jennifer kid who'd just died because of it. A mug's game, drugging, but then Sarah was such a bloody little fool she'd try it 'just for fun'. Christ, the number of times he'd heard her say just that— 'Come on, Larry, just for fun!' Mostly he'd gone along with her, amused to find she'd dare practically anything—ton-ups to pinching road signs to bathing nude in Trafalgar Square fountain; sleeping rough on Hampstead Heath to drinking neat vodka from a tooth tumbler just to prove she could hold her drink. Crazy kid! In a way he was fond of her, admired her courage. She had guts all right, but she was no more right for him than he was for her. In the end, he'd drag her down to his level. That or crack up trying to prove he was better than she.

Well, if they ever got out of this alive, he'd have a chance to set the record straight just this once. He'd ditch her in Cape Town or wherever they landed up and let Daddy come and bail her out. It'd cost him a packet, no doubt. Might even do a stretch for abducting a minor—or as accessory to helping her use a false passport and using one himself. Oh, they'd get him for sure but the publicity he'd get would compensate.

'That's it, Larry!' he thought with sudden disgust. 'Still totting up the cash value of the only decent thing you're ever likely to do.'

And what's so decent about giving up a girl you didn't love? Well, he wanted her. He'd wanted her right from the start. She was something he'd never really believed he could have, even down to the title—or should he say 'up to' the title? She'd been a virgin when he first met her, as innocent as they come, and as upper-class as they come. And she'd taught him, surprisingly, a thing or two about making love. Reared on back-street mating, he'd never known it could be the way it sometimes was with Sarah—kind of sweet and different. He'd almost thought he did love her. But he knew now that he'd only loved what she'd given him.

'Who wants love anyway?' Larry asked himself bitterly. It weakened a guy, softened him up and then there'd come the crunch. He'd learned the hard way not to be soft—it didn't pay. He'd be better off without her—she would only have been a stone around his neck. When he got back, he'd find himself another girl . . .

When he got back? *If* he got back!

In the darkness he grinned. He'd survived diphtheria when he was a year old; he'd survived that knifing incident when he was fourteen when the doctors said he wouldn't make it; he'd survived the craziest of near-misses and not always misses on that first fast bike he'd owned, not to mention the crash on the M1 in his first Jag. He wasn't going to be written off that easily now through no fault of his own. He was the original cat with nine lives and hadn't used the ninth yet.

Beside him, Sarah stirred. She was murmuring in her sleep. He bent his head close to her and made out her sleep-thickened voice:

'Daddy? Is that you, Daddy?'

'To hell with Daddy!' he said, pulling the blanket over her bare arm. 'Everything's okay, Sarah. Go to sleep!' Despite his words, his voice was gentle, protective, kindly. Her lips parted as the tense expression left her face and she settled back into her child's sleep.

Her brother, Andrew, was riding his pony bareback in the paddock. They had fixed up some jumps and were daring each other to take them without saddle or stirrups. Andrew, at fourteen, was Sarah's hero. Tall, clean-cut, he looked every inch the young well-bred English public schoolboy. He was one of those easy-natured, uncomplicated characters who naturally did everything well. Sarah adored him. She'd always adored him from her position of kid sister, two years younger. The fact that their parents loved him more than they loved her didn't bother her in the least. She understood their love from the depths of her own emotions.

Now, in her dream, she stood in the hot August sunshine watching him clear the first three jumps and filled with admiration at the easy way he took them. She was happy. In a minute, she would try to emulate Andrew and fail, of course, to do as well, and he'd come across the field and smile up at her and say: 'Never mind, old girl, you didn't do so badly!'

Then the dream changed, as it always did, to nightmare. The pony missed its footing— slipped, fell—all in slow motion. Sarah stood rooted to the ground, unable to move, watching with horror as the little chestnut mare rolled slowly over on top of Andrew, crushing him . . . crushing the life out of him . . .

She ran, as she once had and still did in her dream, for her father. 'Daddy . . . Daddy . . .' They did not let her go back to the field. She stood at the library window watching, tearless, stunned, as her father came back across the lawn carrying Andrew's body. As she watched, Andrew's arm swung gently to and fro, lifeless yet moving. She looked at her father's face, and knew, with a child's absolute clarity, that her brother was dead.

Now, as she woke, tears coursing down her cheeks, she clung to Larry's comforting arm, knowing it was not Andrew's, nor even her father's but nevertheless still strangely comforting.

'What's wrong?' he whispered. 'Scared?'
'A little!'

He imagined, of course, that she was frightened of dying here in the vastness of the Sahara Desert with all these other strange people. She'd never told him about the dream, the nightmare; nor even about Andrew. Father had forbidden anyone to speak her brother's name in the great big house that was so unbearably empty once Andrew had left it. He'd meant it for the best, knowing how their only son's name affected his grieving wife, but Sarah knew instinctively it was wrong to bury grief. Nevertheless, she buried hers, too, beneath a mad whirl of irresponsible activity. But for the extenuating circumstances of her brother's death, she would have been expelled during that first term back at school. At least her mad behaviour had succeeded in distracting her parents.

Only half aware of how and why she continued to behave in such a fashion, Sarah had continued in this new guise, finding relief for herself whenever depression threatened to overcome her in selecting some dare-devil adventure calculated to make her admiring group of school friends gasp and to absorb her until the mood was over. It was easier, she found, to live this way. She did not want to give herself time to think. Thinking meant that intolerable sense of loss. It meant, too, an equally intolerable sense of inadequacy, for she knew in her heart she could never make up to her parents for the loss of their adored son and heir. At least now no one tried to make her parents think of her in comparable terms. Andrew was the good seed; she, the bad. The harder those in authority sought to mould her, the more fiercely she fought, finally establishing her own total individuality by total defiance of all her family stood for, valued. Larry was but the last in a chain of revolt. Had he been able to evoke, even in the nth degree, the memory of Andrew, she would not have wanted him.

Did she want him? Now, in the darkness, holding his arm, the tears still undried on her cheeks, she knew that she did not. She had never loved any human being since Andrew; never allowed herself to love anyone. The pattern of escape had become a way of life and finding out about sex with Larry had been but an automatic follow-up to the school escapades. She'd spent her life running away and now, suddenly, she didn't want to run any more. If there were only five more days, a week, two weeks, left to live, then she wanted to live them remembering and not forgetting Andrew. She wanted to go back, right back, to their wonderfully uncomplicated, shared childhood: to picnics in the birch woods; to Ludo in the nursery and crumpets for tea; to Christmases and birthdays and those even-better days when Andrew came home from his prep school for the holidays and finding him just the same after all those fears that life in a boys' school might have changed him, altered his affection for her. It never did. Those were the most precious days of all . . .

Sarah's mind, strangely clear, recognised that quite suddenly she had grown up. She wasn't sure why. Perhaps Mrs Carson's death? Or the girl Larry had carried back in his arms reminding her so painfully and terribly of her father carrying Andrew . . . or perhaps just the thought that death was round the corner for her, too. She hadn't thought about dying in a long while. Rejecting a God who could smite Andrew down in his fourteenth year, she had refused confirmation or even to attend church. She'd shocked poor old Nanny with her loud laughter when the old girl had tried to make her see Andrew happily riding his pony in a story-book Heaven with God smiling benignly upon him.

How could Andrew be riding his pony when it was still alive and kicking, silly old fool! In her heart she hadn't wanted Andrew so far away, so out of reach. She hadn't wanted him in the graveyard, either, being eaten by worms.

But now . . . now it was possible to think of a place—a Heaven, where Andrew might be waiting for her the way she'd once waited for him to come back from school. Only she would have changed . . . changed so that he wouldn't know her; probably wouldn't like her much.

She didn't like herself. But if Heaven existed at all, surely it must be a perfect place, and in a perfect place she would be twelve years old again, unspoilt, the way Andrew had loved her? If she could only believe that . . . if really she could believe it, she might even get up now and walk out into the darkness the way that girl had done.

But would she? Did she really want to die? Was Andrew really still so important to her that she'd give up life itself for him? It seemed strangely disloyal even to doubt it, yet she was doubting. She wasn't afraid to die but she wanted to live; not the way she had been living but differently. She wanted to . . . perhaps more than anything else in the world, she wanted to go home; to force herself to walk across the paddock and accept Andrew's death and begin again . . .

Beside her, Larry stirred. Instinctively, she drew away from him and held herself taut, resisting, in the darkness. But gradually her muscles relaxed. It wasn't his fault. None of it was his fault. Tomorrow she'd tell him she couldn't go through with it; couldn't marry him if they did get out of this alive. He would understand. Watching him with that dead girl and the gentle way he'd handed her into her father's arms, she'd seen a different Larry; not hard or uncaring or aggressive but tender, moved deeply by the tragedy. She'd seen him with his defences down and she'd never again be able to believe in the 'Who-gives-a-damn' playboy who had made good.

CHAPTER NINE

The prisoners were becoming something of a problem. Maxwell and Bob had agreed that they should be kept tied up out of harm's way but it was impossible to retain them in the aircraft hold where the daytime heat was intolerable. They had therefore been bound with ropes to the exterior of the plane within sight and sound of the passengers.

At first the three men had been completely ignored. But now the group of Kenyans who constituted the football team were beginning to wander up, possibly from sheer boredom, and bait the prisoners. Angerro complained to Bob that he had been severely kicked and showed an ugly deep gash on one leg.

Whilst Bob had very little sympathy indeed with the men who had brought them to their present situation, he knew that he could not permit his prisoners to be manhandled. They would, if any of them survived, be brought to justice and he could not permit or turn a blind eye to any form of persecution in the meanwhile. On half rations of food and water, their freedom removed, the men were in a fairly pitiable state as it was. There was no fight in them and in Bob's view they would cause little trouble if they were released.

He called a meeting of the committee and the matter was discussed. Bruce suggested a guard be put on the prisoners for their own protection. Kennedy was for releasing them during the daytime and giving them some of the more unpleasant chores that had to be done. There was, for instance, the filling in of the previous day's latrine holes and the digging of new ones at present undertaken by the African footballers. To relieve them of this duty together with the burying of refuse and other such tasks would mollify them and keep the prisoners occupied. They could be secured again at night in the aircraft hold.

The committee supported Maxwell's plan and the three prisoners were released.

'I don't like it!' Bruce told Eve. 'I know they look docile and harmless but I still feel uneasy.'

His fears were not entirely unfounded. Somehow, during the day, one of the men obtained a knife. That night he released his two companions and managed to steal from the food dump half the remaining rations and one of the two precious remaining water cans. The other had been upturned and poured into the sand. When morning came, the men were gone.

It was impossible to keep the disaster from the passengers. John Wilson and Mary-Lou, discovering the scene when they went to the dump for water for the weak coffee which now constituted the party's breakfast, were discreet enough to report the fact in whispers to Bruce and Kennedy. But as Kennedy, white faced, pointed out, they could not keep the facts to themselves. There was no way of hiding from everyone the extent or the consequences of the disaster. They were without water and this would mean a maximum of forty-eight hours of survival; perhaps less for some of the older, frailer members of the party. They were all of them already suffering to some degree from dehydration.

Bob, stifling his own growing horror at the thought of death suddenly so near and so horrible, managed to make the announcement in a cool unpanicked tone. The silence that followed his statement was almost worse than an angry outburst of reaction. No one spoke. Harold Curry reached for his wife's hand and gripped it tightly. Across the aisle, Mrs James started to weep silently. Ted James remained in a stiff upright position, his face stunned as if his mind could not register this further horror following on his daughter's suicide.

The three young hairdressers glanced at one another nervously. Denise produced a packet of cigarettes and paused as Janet whispered:

'Should you smoke? It might make you . . .' she hesitated . . . 'more thirsty.'

They looked quickly away from each other's

eyes. Denise gave a nervous, childish giggle.

'So what!' she said. 'At least it will calm my nerves.'

But the flame on her cigarette lighter went out and Denise made no attempt to flick the switch a second time.

Chris Barlow held his young wife in his arms, no longer caring who saw how he felt about her. He kissed her with a desperate hungry need and resolved that when the time came for them to die, they would walk out into the desert alone together and end their life loving each other. He thought suddenly of the marriage ceremony they had so recently heard—till death us do part. The thought was intolerable to him. Death could not part them. When they were found, they would be clasped together and, pray God, buried together.

Larry Bell was looking at Sarah's face. His first feeling of shock had given way to one of surprise. The kid looked so calm—almost as if the thought of death didn't frighten her. She must, deep down, be as scared as hell. He was. Funny thing about class—girls like Sarah were brought up to hide their emotions and trained to keep their self control in emergencies. He'd read about it but never really believed it till now. She had guts. More than he. He felt his intestines gripping with cold fear. This was a time for a fix if ever there was one and he'd given his stuff to the crazy girl who'd killed herself.

152

'What are you thinking about?' he asked. 'Scared?'

Sarah looked at him with vague startled eyes.

'I suppose so, yes! I was thinking of my brother . . . he died, you know, when I was twelve. I was wondering—well, I suppose it sounds daft to you, but I was wondering if I'd see him—you know, if there was somewhere we all go—Heaven or something.'

'Wish to Christ I could believe that!' Larry said, taking a deep breath and expelling the air slowly from his lungs. 'Never did take much to religion—wasn't time for it when I was a kid. We were too busy trying to make out in this life to be bothered about the next. Didn't know you'd had a brother. You never said.'

'No. I loved him. More than anyone in the whole world.'

Something in her tone made him look at her a second time. Her face was young, shining, very beautiful . . . and infinitely sad.

'I don't know her,' he thought. 'I've been with her, slept with her, bloody nearly married her and I don't know the first thing about her. Funny, really. Now it's too late but I'd really like to know her. Might even find myself loving her. Haven't loved anyone really—not ever. Except myself, maybe!' He grinned.

'Are you laughing at me?'

'God, no!' he told her. 'Laughing at myself, I suppose. I was thinking what a right selfish bastard I'd been all my life. I never cared about anything—except making good—or making girls. I'd be different—at least I think so, if we ever got out of this bloody desert.'

'Then you think there is still some hope?'

He was about to shake his head but now, suddenly, he wanted to make it easier for her, if he could. At least he could end his life a bit less selfishly than he'd lived it.

'Course there is!' he lied. 'Stands to reason they'll be out looking for us and every day that's passed and they haven't found us elsewhere, the greater our chances they'll start looking in this direction.'

'But why should they?' Sarah argued logically. 'We're not on the route we should have been flying. I was talking to the co-pilot yesterday. He told me we'd been forced off course.'

Larry was shaken. He hadn't known that. He managed a smile.

'So what? We aren't depending on search planes. There's all those travelling Arabs— what do you call them—Bedouins. They'll be around this part of the world and spot us stuck here. You should be able to see this ruddy great plane for miles and miles with the sun reflecting off it. Like a bloody beacon we must be in the daytime. God knows the terrain's flat enough . . . nothing to deflect the reflection. It wouldn't surprise me if they'd seen us days ago, but don't forget they travel on foot or camels or something; take 'em time to get here.'

'Oh, Larry!' Sarah said, her voice suddenly soft and without a trace of its usual brittleness. 'What a comforting thought. You are a funny person—quite different, really, to what I thought you were like. If any of the gang asked me if you'd know anything about Bedouins or angles of reflection, I'd have bet a million pounds the answer would have been "no".'

His smile met her own.

'Can't claim an education I never had,' he told her. 'I only know about the desert from the film *Lawrence of Arabia*. And as for light reflections—well, they're much the same as sound and I know about that from the electric amplifiers and such we use in the group. I picked up quite a bit of info from the technicians when we were making our recordings. Sounds daft, I suppose, but I was tempted to do some night classes on electrical engineering. That's what I wanted to be once—when I was at school—an engineer. But I never did get an education to speak of. Dad reckoned it was a waste of time cultivating brains when it was sheer brawn made him his money. Bit pig-headed, my Dad, though to give him his due, he went along with it when I wanted to start the group. Saw the cash benefits, I suppose. After that, I never had time to get educated. Never thought about it much—till I took up with you.'

'Me!' Sarah repeated. 'I'm a complete

moron!'

'You're not, you know. You were always surprising me—suddenly talking French or German like they was your own language; and the things you seemed to know about foreign countries and the way you always had words for things you wanted to say. Often hadn't a bloody clue what you were talking about but I'd never admit it. You taught me a lot. I'm grateful.'

Sarah reached out her hand in an involuntary and unconscious gesture and touched the nape of his neck in a strange little caress.

'Life is odd!' she said gently. 'I did not realise that you were—the way you are. I always thought of you as terribly sophisticated, knowledgeable about life. You bluffed your way along very well, Larry. I never knew despite the fact that we . . .'

She broke off, suddenly unaccountably shy.

'Were strangers in the night,' he broke in and then grinned, adding: 'We had some daytime sessions too, though, didn't we?'

They smiled at each other, intimate now in shared memory.

'I wish . . . well, I don't mean this the way it might sound, Sarah, but I hope like hell we do get out of this. I want . . . I want another chance . . . with you, I mean. To get to know you . . . Forget what's gone and start again as if we'd only just met. Sarah . . . love's not something I know much about—the kind of love you see on films and that. Always seemed kind of soft to me. You wanted a bird—you had her, if you could get her; maybe you liked her, maybe you didn't. How long it lasted depended how well you hit it off—sexwise, I mean. With us—well, it was good, wasn't it?'

She nodded, her face averted, listening. She'd never heard Larry talk so seriously before.

'I guess that seemed enough when you first started talking about getting hitched. Yet deep down, can't explain it really, I wasn't for marriage. I respected you all right—wanted you all right—but being tied for life—didn't seem right, really, though I couldn't have told you why. I reckon there's more to it—you've got to care—want it right for her more than you do for yourself; want to look after her; that kind of thing. Maybe we won't get out of this mess and that's why I'm trying to get the record straight. I liked you a lot, Sarah, but I wouldn't ever have married you except to prove I wasn't chicken. And I know that's wrong now. Sounds daft?'

She smiled at him, a warm friendly smile.

'Not in the least. It sounds honest. It was the same with me. I think I wanted to defy my parents, shock them. I thought—no, that's just the point, I didn't think. I didn't want to think. I've tried for years and years to fill my life so full of action that I didn't have to think. With you and the gang—well, it was just one mad

157

giggle, wasn't it? I was using you, Larry—using you because I didn't want to be made to face up to life. I didn't do it consciously. But I wasn't in love with you either. I don't know what it's like to be "in love" but I *did* know what loving meant and I didn't want to love anyone after Andrew died. It hurts too much when you lose them. I've been a coward. I want to get out of this alive, too, Larry. I want to live. I want to love, too, and fall in love. I don't want to die.'

With no other thought in his mind but to comfort her, Larry put his arms around her and held her close. In front of him, he could see Chris Barlow comforting his young wife in the same way and also the old-age pensioners. He felt the sharp sting of tears behind his eyes.

'Christ!' he thought, 'I haven't cried since I was a nipper and that daft mongrel of mine was flattened by the dustcart down our street. Must be going soft!'

But he didn't take his arms away and felt strangely happy when Sarah pushed closer against him, drawing from him what comfort she could.

Only the Africans took the news badly. After the first shock wore off, they surged round Kennedy and Bob talking in high, angry voices. They wanted to go after the prisoners.

'We are fit—fitter than they!' one of the younger men said eagerly. 'We would catch them up by evening. We could split up into four groups and one lot would reach them.'

They wanted retribution—and a return of the stolen water and food. But Kennedy knew it was pointless.

'You'd be risking your lives for nothing!' he told them. 'Don't you see? They are bound to die out there somewhere, sooner or later. When death comes, it'll be harder for them. They can't walk far in this heat, in the condition they're in, even with the water and food they took. We are hundreds of miles from civilisation. They have no shelter, no shade. Walking, their water supply won't last a day. Leave them. Forget them. Save your strength as much as possible. The less movement, the less tension, the less effort you make, the longer your bodies will survive and the greater your chances of rescue.'

Gradually he soothed the men down to a sullen acquiescence. He was glad that they did not try to take the law into their own hands, for he could not have stopped them. During the past few days, they had grown naturally to accept his authority. So long as they continued to do so, he could protect them from themselves—perhaps even save their lives.

As they had said, they were accustomed to the intense heat and would suffer the deprivations less than their European companions. Their chances of survival were the greater if he could keep them from panicking.

Already thirst was assailing all of them.

They had had no water since the third of a small plastic cupful that had been their last ration before bed the previous night. The plane was beginning to heat up as the rays of the morning sun beat down on it. He ordered everyone out into the shade and told them to lie quietly so as to conserve their body fluids.

At mid-day, no one seemed inclined to eat, despite their hunger. They were too thirsty, their mouths too parched and dry to be able to face the thought of eating a few biscuits which might absorb what little moisture was still in their mouths. There were still half a dozen apples in the food store. Kennedy, at Eve's suggestion, agreed they should be divided into small portions and each person given a tiny segment to suck.

'Wonder if they come from Kent!' John said to Mary-Lou who was lying with her head in his lap, her pretty dark hair spread across his bare knees. It was his home county and he was passionately attached to his home there.

'More likely come from Australia!' Mary-Lou replied in an attempt not to let John's thoughts become too nostalgic. She knew the temptation. Her own home was on the Cornish coast and time and again her imagination had carried her back to the sound of the mountains of water rushing into great cool caves and gurgling out again. Water—even salt water— would be like a miracle now. Just to be able to dabble her feet in one of those clear shining rock pools! To plunge her hot sticky arms into the waving wet green seaweed . . . to dive her head, face first, into one of the surfing breakers and . . .

'John, first thing I want to do when I get back to England is to take you home with me—to Cornwall. You'll come, won't you? Meet Mum and Dad and old John, the lobster catcher, who was my first love, before you.'

He ran a finger through a lock of her hair, smiling.

'No, first thing I buy a ring and we get ourselves engaged—officially. Then Cornwall.'

Bruce looked into Eve's large grey eyes. They seemed in this haze of heat to be like twin pools of cool quiet water. Staring into them, he could imagine himself slipping deeper and deeper into their cool depths, drowning slowly, sensuously, the water closing softly over his head, his burning body turning icy cold. The surface of the water shimmered, broke up and he could no longer see his own reflection. Eve was smiling.

'You were staring at me, darling, as if . . . as if . . .'

'I was about to die?' he finished for her as she broke off embarrassed by her thoughtless words. 'Well, maybe I am, Eve, and God knows I haven't had much of a chance in my lifetime to look at you. You are one of the loveliest women I've ever seen. Serene, beautiful, calm.'

'Not really!' Eve said quietly. 'Not inside,

I'm feeling more than I've ever felt anything in my whole life. Not just cravings like thirst but regrets, too. I've wasted so much of my life feeling injured and hurt and bitter—never appreciating all the good things I did have. And now there's you . . . and most of all I don't want to die because of you. I regret this lost chance of happiness with you. Oh, Bruce, tell me honestly—suppose the trip had gone exactly to schedule—suppose we'd landed that night at Cairo and you'd disembarked for the Cairo talks and I'd flown on to South Africa. Would we have seen each other again? Ever?'

Now Bruce was smiling.

'You bet we would. I'd have been haunted by your memory; I would have had to get to know you; find out what you were really like under that beautiful calm exterior; if you were my sort of woman or cold and hard and unresponsive. Maxwell and I had planned a three-day holiday after the talks. I'd have spent them finding you.'

'And am I your sort of woman?'

He gave her a look of quick intensity.

'You know that you are—in every way. Last night . . . I lay awake looking out at the desert bathed in moonlight. I had a desperate urge to come along to the galley where you and Mary-Lou were sleeping and wake you up and take you out there and make violent love to you. I kept thinking of that first night we went out there and wondering how in hell I stopped myself from doing so. It was the same reason I didn't wake you last night. I love you. I don't want anything to be other than perfect for you. Now, this minute, I am wondering if I was crazy. I might die now never having loved you fully. It seems so silly that we did not when we could . . .'

'I know what you mean,' Eve said gravely. 'But I don't think it was silly. I think it was all exactly right. Whether there's an ending or not, at least we started right. I'm grateful.'

Not far away, Maxwell Kennedy sat writing to his wife.

I'm grateful, darling, he wrote, *for everything you gave me, did for me, meant to me. I'm grateful for all the love and for all your many hundreds of loving kindnesses. I'm grateful for all the moments of pure joy, for your companionship, your help, your friendship. Except for the unhappiness I know my death will cause you, I don't feel that I have been cheated of my life for I lived it fully, perfectly and wonderfully with you. I regret nothing but that I have to leave you. If when you read this you are sad, as I know you will be, try not to give way to sorrow. You know how your tears would grieve me and if one can see one's loved ones after death, then I would wish to see you happy, my dearest.*

Whatever you may read about this adventure, do not imagine any of the horrors newspaper men may write. We are not suffering, are not

163

injured nor in pain, only thirsty and that is not so hard to bear. It will come quickly at the end and I know that we are fortunate not to be lost on the sea without shelter or shade and the opportunity to die privately without horror to those around. It could have been a long-drawn-out slow going which cannot be the case in this situation. I shall die in peace and at peace. I shall die as I lived, loving you . . .

Well, part of it was true. The end would come quickly. But not painlessly. Nor was he without regret. He had always enjoyed life, enjoyed his work and would be leaving it at a time when many of his labours were coming to fruition. He would be leaving Nancy at a time when retirement was not far off and he could cease travelling the world and enjoy the life they'd so often planned and looked forward to. He'd been going to buy a small ranch in California, up in the hills away from the crowds and the publicity and demands of civilisation.

His gaze wandered from the writing pad on his knee to Bruce and Eve. He felt guilty at his own self-pity. These young ones were those for whom he should keep his pity—the ones who had never known, or only briefly, the happiness that marriage to a living, good woman could mean; for Bruce in particular, who had been lonely far too long and who deserved happiness. It was good to see him looking happy, especially at a time like this. He was grateful to Eve.

The afternoon wore on—the heat intensifying and then as darkness fell swiftly as it did in the desert, suddenly cooling. For a few moments, the cool air seemed to soothe their aching throats and burning tongues, but the sensation did not last.

By morning several members of the party were in bad shape. Elsie Curry was too weak to stand; her husband gasping as if he could not get his breath. Kennedy wondered if they would last the day. One of the Africans had disappeared in the night—no one knew where and none had the strength now to search for him. Young Liz Barlow gave way to the terror and horror of the situation and became hysterical but was calmed eventually by Eve and Mary-Lou helping her frantic husband with soothing cheerful words that they had difficulty in voicing, so parched were their throats.

Edith Hurst was the next casualty, fainting as she walked the few yards back to the shade of the plane from the latrine. Everyone was now in pain as their stomachs knotted with hunger. It had become almost impossible to swallow solid food and there was nothing with which to unsolidify it. One of the three young hairdressers was burning with a high fever and delirious.

Bob crawled across the few yards of sand separating him from Kennedy.

'If they don't find us today, it'll be too late!' he said through cracked and swollen lips.

Kennedy met his eyes levelly.

'Yes, I'm afraid so!' he agreed.

CHAPTER TEN

It was the youngest son of the kadi who found the black, fly-covered bodies of the Nigerian prisoners. He was hunting for lizards amongst the rocks when the stench of death assailed his aquiline little nose.

Curiosity sent him in search of the reason for such an odour. His brown, intelligent little face screwed up in surprise when he came upon the men. He stared for a time, plucked up courage to remove from one body a shining wrist watch, and turning, ran back to where the tents were grouped in a small cluster in the wide wastes of sand.

His father, the kadi, listened at first with disbelief to the child's story and then, seeing the watch, hurried the boy to the Sheikh's tent.

Yes, the men were dead! The child answered the questions showered on him. He was familiar enough with death. It did not frighten him. Yes, they were black as charred wood, not brown like themselves. Never had he seen men like them. They were not like white men though they wore European clothing. They had been dead at least one full day.

Puzzled, as curious as the child, his elders set out in a group to see for themselves these strange dead men. It was puzzling, for no member of their tribe had ever seen a human being this deep in the desert unless he were, like themselves, one of the true Bedouin nomads, and they buried their dead.

When, a short time later, they stood in a circle round the three sun-scorched bodies, they saw that the boy spoke the truth. These were neither Arabs nor white men, but were from some unknown tribe.

They studied the dead men's material possessions—the Sheikh appropriating a knife that lay glinting in the sun. Nearby lay a black BOAC bag, incongruously civilised in the great wastes of sand.

'There is a bird painted upon it!' said the boy, pointing to the wings. He knew of the existence of great mechanical birds flown by men high up in the sky from one horizon to the next, even beyond the sun's setting and the moon's rising places. Were these men from the sky?

The Sheikh seemed to think well of this explanation. The kadi looked at his young son with pride. The boy had wits sharper than most.

A counsel followed from which the child was excluded. A search began to trace the trail along which the dead men had walked to their deaths. Their footprints, undisturbed by wind or sand, led far into the distance across the shimmering dunes.

It was decided by the Bedouins that they would return to camp, eat and when the sun grew cooler, move on, following the path of the footprints.

An hour passed and another. Pipes were smoked and the talk amongst the men was only surpassed by the talk amongst the women. Speculation as to what might be found at the end of the track gave excitement to an otherwise severe and eventless existence. Much of their time was spent in the telling of tales but to the older members of the tribe, most of these stories were too well known to have any novelty. Imagination was now given free reign. Here indeed was a tale! And the ending still in abeyance.

They moved off two hours before sunset, the boy running ahead eagerly pointing out again and again the clear signs of the men's long walk from the crashed plane. Now and again there were telltale marks of their journey, the empty water can, the hollow where they had fallen exhausted to rest. Further still, discarded clothing, a piece of orange peel which the child picked up and chewed, savouring the flavour.

As darkness fell, swiftly and intense, they rested. Women fed their babies. The goats were milked. Then, as the moon rose, brilliant, silvery and incandescent, they moved on, bound by their child-like curiosity and imagination, to find the end of the trail.

Before dawn they stopped to sleep, not troubling to pitch their tents for they would be on the move again in an hour or two. The boy, exhausted with excitement, was not the first to rouse. One of the women, waking to the cry of her baby, stood up as the sun burst over the horizon and was first to see the strange flash of silver far away to the west. She watched, forgetting the hungry wails of the child, seeing only the strange bright light shift and dart and flash as the sun moved higher. Then she ran to wake her husband.

Within minutes the whole camp was astir, all looking towards the great dazzle of silver light, brighter even than the moon. The boy, like many others, was agog to go forward at once but this was forbidden until they had eaten. The meal of rice and dried lizard was soon finished and at last the tribe moved forward, westward in the direction of the plane.

*   *   *

For some time Bruce was aware of voices. He had been suffering all day from such fevered fantasies that at first he took no notice. He was no longer sure what was real and what was illusion brought on by approaching death. That morning Elsie Curry had died. Soon after her husband had collapsed. One of the Africans had killed himself with a knife. No one had had strength enough to bury the dead. By mid-day nearly everyone was in a coma, experiencing long bursts of unconsciousness broken by occasional bouts of sanity and a torturing awareness of thirst. No one hoped any longer—except that death would come quickly and end their agony.

It was the baby's cry which at last made Bruce force open his red-rimmed eyes and try to focus his wavering sight in the direction of the sound. He believed then that he was dreaming again, delirious. A number of people, white robed, brown of face, were standing grouped on the edge of their pathetic patch of shade beneath the plane's wing. One man, taller than the rest, more imposing, noticed the slight movement of Bruce's eyes and stepped forward. He stood silently staring down at Bruce. With a desperate effort Bruce tried to speak. His lips, cracked, swollen, dried into black rims, refused to open. The Arab bent over him, put the nozzle of a goatskin water bag to his mouth.

He closed his eyes. It had to be a dream—a dream he wanted to last for ever and ever. Water. Again he tasted water.

He heard a voice. Was it his own? No, Kennedy's. What was he saying? He tried to listen, to concentrate.

'For God's sake, Bruce, listen to me. They're here. The Bedouins are here. Bruce, can you hear me? Bruce!'

The women were plundering the plane, their voices shrill with excitement as they sorted through clothes, jewellery, handbags, blankets, shining objects from the galley, cups, pots, pans. They were like children set loose in a toy shop from which they could choose their fancy at will. They had never set eyes on such riches or even imagined them. They were ready to protect these new treasures with their lives.

It was Kennedy's knowledge of Arabic which saved the lives of those who could still be saved amongst the victims of the crash. He managed somehow to make the Sheikh understand that great wealth would be his if he helped them, gave them water, succoured them. One of the tribe must be sent for help, no matter how long it took to reach civilisation. Then, he promised, a great plane would come and shower wealth upon the Sheikh, silver in large bags if he wished it, food, tents, animals—anything he wanted. If he let them die or killed them, then he would have only what he saw here and that was as nothing beside the riches that would be his if he helped them.

Then he collapsed, too exhausted by the effort of speech to cling any longer to his last shreds of strength to wait for the outcome of the Sheikh's counsel.

It was night-time when Eve woke. A young dark-skinned girl was sitting beside her smiling. As Eve's eyes opened, the girl dampened her mouth with water and gave her a warm sweet drink. She fell asleep again almost immediately. Next time she woke, it was daylight. Again she was given drink—only a little, but her body felt easier. Looking down, she saw that her skin was shining with oil. The smell was unpleasant but the lubrication of the oil on her parched skin was so indescribably soothing she did not care. She was given yet another cupful of warm goat's milk. It was the most marvellous drink she had ever had and she was conscious enough now to know that for the rest of her life, no other drink would ever be as good again.

It was then that she became more fully aware of her existence. She was alive! Her eyes ached but there was not sufficient liquid in her body for her to cry. She turned her head and saw Mary-Lou, sleeping; young Liz Barlow drinking from a cup; Sarah smiling weakly in her direction. She realised they were in a tent. The air smelt of the oil that covered her. Outside the sun blazed upon the tiny particles of sand. She closed her eyes, unwilling to see the desert.

When it was dark she woke again. More goat's milk was given her. She opened her eyes and drank to the dregs of the cup and then looked up to see Bruce sitting watching her.

'The women didn't want me to see you,' he said, each word coming through cracked lips with extreme difficulty. 'Men in this tribe are not allowed in women's tents.' His face contorted into a painful smile. 'So I said we were married!'

He held her hand, their two oily palms sticking together in blissful happiness.

'Tell me who . . . who else made it?' she asked him.

But he would only say:

'Most of us, darling. Go back to sleep now. We're okay!'

Ten days later the news was flashed around the world that the missing V.C. 10 was rumoured to have been sighted in the Sahara Desert. There were said to be some survivors. The whole world waited for the follow-up. Two weeks earlier, every newspaper had carried the story that the giant aeroplane with the American diplomat Kennedy Maxwell on board was overdue. Like a serial in a magazine came the next report that it was thought to be down in the Mediterranean. Speculation mounted. Was it sabotage? How important a man was Maxwell? Life stories of the two young stewardesses appeared. The story touched the headlines again when it became known that the pop singer Larry Bell was on board. Teenage fans sent hysterical letters to the club and Larry's group members were interviewed on TV and asked if they would continue without him.

Someone told a reporter that the teenage daughter of Lord Finnon-Waters had been eloping with Larry Bell, that the police were looking into the question of forged passports.

Nancy Maxwell was photographed hiding her face from the cameras as she stepped off a plane from Washington at Cairo Airport. The story of the Pools win by the three young hairdressers was told by their distraught parents. Meanwhile, a gigantic land and sea search was still in operation, hampered by no hint of disaster from the radio of the missing plane. No one really knew where to search. The plane had vanished completely.

In London, at Heathrow, a man named Peter, unshaven, exhausted, unknown, pestered every possible official hourly for news of Mrs Leanora Carson. In Cairo, Granville Carson bore up under the strain with a stiff upper lip and told his Brigadier that he would face the worst like a man. In England, a priest remembered Leanora Carson's name and said a prayer for her, bowing his head and accepting God's will and regretted that it had to be done this way.

In South Africa, Celia wept and hoped alternately until the search was called off and weeping, she accepted the fact that she would now never see her parents again. She tried, but could not bring herself to tell her children they would not see their grandparents after all.

In a large silent mansion in Sussex, Lord Finnon-Waters faced his wife across the breakfast table and when hope was abandoned, finally broke his vow of silence.

'We never loved her—not the way we loved Andy!' he said, speaking his son's name for the first time since his death. 'Perhaps it was our fault she turned out as wild as she was. Nanny always said it was Sarah, not Andy, who had the softest heart. I thought I never wanted to see her again when she ran off that day; I thought I didn't care what became of her. But I do. I did. I do care . . .'

Nanny sat in the nursery in the rocking chair, her face puffy with weeping. First Andy. Now Sarah: There was no one now. Poor little Sarah, always wanting to be noticed and no one but her to see. Now she *was* being noticed and it was all to no purpose. Her sweet little face shone off the centre page of the *Sunday Mirror*, looking so young and happy and alive. What would have happened to Sarah if she'd lived—running off like that with that long-haired pop singer? And them downstairs, making Sarah a Ward of Court . . .

Nanny wept on. She thought of that other nanny on the plane. How she would have envied Edith Hurst going out to a new life in Cairo, though she'd felt sympathy when she'd read in the paper that she had no relatives worrying or grieving for her. If they had been rescued, she would have written to Miss Hurst—yes, she'd made up her mind to it—written to say she was glad she was safe. It wasn't right not having anyone to care.

Nancy Maxwell sat in the lounge of Shepheard's Hotel in Cairo, knitting a grey golf jersey. She wanted to finish it in time for Kennedy's birthday next month. Sitting here, day after day, she'd completed the body and was on the second sleeve.

'I don't know how you can sit there, knitting!' said her friend, Julia, who had flown over with her to lend her support and give her comfort if the worst happened. She hadn't meant to speak in such a way to Nancy but her own nerves had been strung to breaking point with the continual lack of news and now, this morning, when they'd said 'No hope', she expected Nancy to break down that terrible reserve. How *could* she stay so calm? So unmoved? Nancy, who everyone knew was as crazy about Maxwell as she'd been the day she married him.

'Because I've got to fill in the time somehow and I might as well be knitting,' Nancy answered. 'I know you think I'm behaving inhumanly, Julia, but you don't understand. I know he's alive. I *know* it. I don't care what they say. I'd know if he was dead. So I'm waiting. Sooner or later they'll find them. You go on back home if you want to. I'll be quite all right. I mean that, Julia. I'm all right.'

Julia sighed. The whole world accepted that there was 'no hope', but not Nancy. It was heartbreaking to watch, Nancy was cushioned from grief by the irrational certainty that Kennedy was still alive; by the conviction that she would know if anything had happened to him. Julia was sure that her friend just couldn't face the truth. But in the end she would have to. Then she would break and Julia knew she must be there to pick up the pieces. If Nancy would only prepare herself . . .

'It's been two weeks. Don't you see, dear, if they'd crashed somewhere on land, someone would have come across the plane by now. If it was in the sea . . . well . . .'

'Don't go on, Julia,' Nancy broke in quietly. 'I know I must sound unreasonable. The odds are a hundred to one against my being right but nothing can alter how I feel . . . here . . .' She placed a hand over her heart. 'I'd know if he was dead. I'd know.'

When the first trickle of news came through, Julia was nearly incoherent with excitement. A phone call had come from the American Embassy.

'They wanted me to break it to you gently, Nancy. There has been a rumour a Bedouin Arab found a plane in the Sahara Desert. It seems there might be some survivors. Mr Wallace begged me to warn you not to set too much store on this, honey. It is just a rumour

177

and they are still waiting for confirmation. Oh, Nancy, suppose it *is* them? Suppose Kennedy is alive?'

Almost immediately it was officially confirmed that a plane with a number of survivors had been found in the Sahara Desert. A small spotter plane had left Tripoli with the Bedouin on board to establish an exact location so that a rescue plane could be flown in. An Arab spokesman, interviewed by Alan Potts, a Tripoli reporter, gave a clear account of the Bedouin's statement. The man described the plane as 'large and silver—big enough to hold all his tribe. It had many wonders in it, seats, doors, windows, blankets, many pretty things.' His tribe were caring for the men and women who were still alive. All the women were white. Some of the men were black. He and his tribe had found three black men dead in the desert some distance from the plane. Some men and some women were dead. His people were doing what they could to feed and care for the living but they did not have big supplies of food or water. The survivors were being given goat's milk as they could not eat. Many could not talk. Some were very ill . . .

Beyond this information and his name, he could say nothing more, except that the white Sheikh had promised his Sheikh great reward.

There was little doubt in anyone's mind now that this was the V.C.10. It remained only to know who were the survivors, who had died. And later, why the plane had come down in the Sahara—so far off course, said a BOAC spokesman, as to be quite incomprehensible.

Reporters and newsmen swarmed onto the next plane to Tripoli. Hospital beds were made ready. Medical men were interviewed as to their opinions on survival in the desert. BOAC were interviewed as to what food, water and medical supplies their V.C.10s carried. Larry's group appeared without him on the David Frost programme. Celia showed her children all the photographs she had of herself with 'Granny and Grandpa'. Lord Finnon-Waters wrote out a huge cheque as a reward for the Bedouin tribe. Nanny switched off the wireless and went to the kitchen to fill hot-water bottles and put them in Sarah's bed to be sure it would be properly aired for her home-coming.

Nancy drew the wool through the last few stitches where she had cut off at the neck edge of a raglan sleeve and sent Julia out to book seats on the next plane to Tripoli.

Granville Carson calculated the odds on Leanora's survival in such circumstances. Her health had never been good. He doubted if she could have survived, but felt in duty bound to go to Tripoli to meet the rescue plane. He obtained leave from his Brigadier.

The editor of a national newspaper allocated large sums of money for 'human interest' stories from the survivors, no holds barred.

CHAPTER ELEVEN

Sarah lay on her stomach propped up by her elbows, chin in hand staring into the flickering flames of the huge log fire. Larry was lying full length on the chintz-covered sofa, the two King Charles spaniels curled up beside him. Radio London filled the room with its familiar modern beat. Neither was listening.

'You know,' Sarah said dreamily, 'the most fantastic thing of all, Larry, the most improbable happening of the whole incredible episode isn't what went on out there in the desert. It's what it's done to everyone. We're different—you, me, Mummy, Daddy—most of all Daddy. I was staggered enough when he said you could come and recuperate here at home but when he let Nanny put you in Andrew's room . . .'

Larry sighed sleepily. Strange how much sleep he seemed to have needed ever since they got back from Tripoli . . . and here in this house there was peace.

'Why so odd?' he asked, feeling Sarah's need to elaborate. He didn't mind her chatter . . . her voice was pretty, attractive to listen to, even if a lot of what she had to say was meaningless. Every now and again she talked sense.

'Well, Andrew's room was shut up after his death. No one was ever allowed to go in there. I did, of course. I knew where Daddy kept the key and I used to pinch it from his study and go up there sometimes when I was a kid and felt lonely.'

'Morbid, weren't you?' Larry said matter-of-factly. He was strangely touched and didn't want to show it. Somehow, since he'd been in hospital he'd lost the ability to be as tough as he wanted. In fact, he'd horrified himself by crying when that rescue plane finally touched down. He didn't feel up to facing publicity. This was the main reason why he had jumped at Sarah's suggestion that he go home with her, if her parents would allow it. He could stay there incognito. Of course, he wanted publicity. He'd be crazy not to want it. Money would flow in and his agent was hopping mad to get him back to London and give him the okay to accept all the offers that were flying around. In a day or two he'd go. Meanwhile well, it was nice here in this crummy old house. Like something you read about in books—smelly old dogs and chintzy furniture and that nanny fussing over him as if he were four years old. Reminded him of Mum. Hadn't thought of her in years, poor old thing. She'd died so long ago, but once she'd fussed over him just the same—'Eat your dinner, lad, it'll put weight on you.' 'Time you was in bed, Larry. Won't grow up big and strong like your Dad if you don't never get no sleep!'

Then there was Sarah's Mum—quite different—all twin sets and pearls and always seemed to be putting flowers in vases all over the house and a bit the grand lady with him, though he was beginning to think this was just shyness. They hadn't much to say to each other so they just smiled over the kippers at breakfast—kippers! Might have been the East End! In a funny way, he felt sorry for her. She didn't seem able to get close to Sarah, either, though you could tell she was fond of her by her voice. That's the only way it showed. She never kissed or hugged her.

The old man was a card—bit like Sarah in a way—all temper and tantrums when he was thwarted and nice as apple pie when things were going his way. Bossy as hell, but then what else would you expect from a Lord? Had a sense of humour, though. They'd had a bit of a laugh about Larry's appearance. The old boy hadn't realised he'd had his hair cut to assume the guise of Henry Bard, clerk, and didn't recognise him in the hospital in Tripoli. Said Sarah could have him back to stay before he found out he was Larry Bell, the degenerate beardie-weirdie he'd been trying to keep his daughter away from! Wouldn't go back on his word, though, and now . . . well, they were almost friends. Said he'd take him pheasant shooting at the weekend.

'That's an honour, Larry—he never shoots with anyone he doesn't like!' Sarah told him. Funny, but he'd felt quite proud—same sort of feeling of 'having made it' as he'd felt when that first record had hit the top twenty.

He sighed again. Life was peculiar. There was so much more to it than he'd ever realised before the crash. He wondered if he could ever get back to the old life—the not knowing or caring much about anything except success. It wasn't going to be easy. He didn't know if he could ever take life itself for granted now— things like a drink of water. Probably would, in time.

Sarah's hair was tied back in a pony tail. She looked fourteen. Acted it, too, most of the time, hauling him off to that old nursery of hers to play Ludo of all things! Showing him toys Nanny had stacked neatly in the toy cupboard and talking endlessly about the way she and that brother of hers had done this and that. It got on his nerves a bit the way she kept on about that Andrew but then he suddenly realised she was saying all the things she hadn't been able to say before and getting it out of her system. Now, a week later, she didn't mention him much. This afternoon was the first time in twenty-four hours and she didn't harp on the subject.

He lay watching the firelight flicker on her smooth unlined cheeks and quietly accepted the fact that he'd been a bit jealous of the brother. He would have liked to hear Sarah talk about him, Larry, in that same warm, affectionate, admiring tone. He wanted her to like him, respect him, need him. Hell, he wanted her to love him!

The thought brought him wide awake.

'Must be daft,' he told himself. 'Doesn't make sense. She's a kid, an empty, pig-headed crazy kid. She's not for me.

'But why not?' he asked himself. 'I could look after her. She needs someone to look after her—someone with a bit more realistic attitude to life. We'd be good for each other—as good that way as it was for us both in bed . . .'

He felt his body stiffening in sudden memory. It was hard to understand but those mad, wild sexual orgies he'd once had with her didn't seem real—more like dreams of what might be than memories of what had been. She didn't look old enough, silly kid, for sex. Yet she was all woman. He knew it. Could it be like that again?

'What are you thinking about. Larry? You're awfully quiet!'

'Oh, but orfully!' he parodied her upper-class accent to hide his sudden obliterating shyness.

She grinned. 'No, seriously. I want to know. You are quiet—not like you used to be at all.'

'Boring you am I?' he said, trying to keep

his tone light.

'No, you're not!' Sarah said almost angrily, tossing her pony tail. 'But I hate being shut out. What were you thinking?'

'What a stupid, useless kid you are!'

He had meant only to tease but to his consternation saw the tears fill her eyes and run down her cheeks. Instantly he was down on the floor beside her, trying incompetently to wipe the tears that were now flowing even faster. He put his arms round her and she clung to him, sobbing like the child she was.

'Oh, don't, Sarah, please! I was only teasing, I swear it. I love you. I really do love you, daft as it sounds. Sarah, are you listening? Oh, Sarah . . .' he broke off helplessly.

The tears were still falling but she was staring at him now, her face screwed up in a frown. Her voice was still choked with tears as she said:

'Do you know what you s-said? You said . . . you said you l-loved me!'

She sounded so astonished that despite his emotion, Larry grinned.

'So what? Anything so terrible in that?'

She drew one long shuddering intake of breath and then melted against him, soft, warm arms winding round his neck and small, sensuous little body pressed against him. He felt his heart leap.

'Oh, Larry!' she said, 'I was afraid it was just me—me that loved you, I mean. I kept telling myself not to pay any attention to the way I felt about you—it was sort of reaction from the accident or something. But I knew I was in love with you that day Daddy arrived at the hospital in Tripoli. I was in the middle of asking him if you could come and stay and suddenly I knew that I'd just die if he said no. And then you came to see me in my ward and I had to wait to find out if you'd say yes, you'd come and you sounded so . . . so uncaring what you did. I was sure you were just coming home with me to get away from the reporters and crowds and everything—not because you wanted to be with me the way I wanted you here all to myself. Oh, Larry, when did you know? Are you sure? Why do you love me? How do you know?'

He held her away from him, staring at her with amused eyes.

'Well, give us a chance. Which question do you want me to answer first? When I knew I loved you? Can't answer. Maybe ages ago when I first took up with you against my better judgement! Maybe just a minute ago when I was looking at you dreaming into the fire. I don't know. But I am sure and I do love you and I do know it's for real. Okay?'

Her eyes were full of happiness—and excited mischief.

'Larry, I'm so happy. We'll get married, won't we? I'll make you a good wife, I swear I will. I'll learn to cook and sew and things.

186

Nanny will teach me. I'm not very domesticated but . . .'

'Who wants a domesticated wife? I certainly don't!'

'Well, I'll learn anyway. Larry, we nearly did it once—we could elope, couldn't we? Only properly this time!'

'No!' he said firmly. 'We could but we won't. This time, we're going to do everything differently. I said out there in that bloody desert that we began wrong and if ever we got out, I wanted to start again right. Well, that's how it's going to be. I'll ask your dad's permission to marry you. He mightn't like it and I don't blame him for thinking I'm not good enough for you but at least I can afford to keep you in the manner to which you are accustomed. Then we'll have a real posh white wedding in that church up the road you showed me last week; and Nanny can be chief bridesmaid!'

When she stopped laughing, Sarah kissed him. With a typical change of mood she became serious again. 'Larry, suppose Daddy says no? Suppose he won't let us?'

'Well, he'll have to, because that's how it's going to be,' Larry said. 'Besides, I somehow don't think he will say no. Best ask him before my hair grows any longer because it'll never be this short again.'

'I should hope not!' said Sarah, running her hand up the nape of his neck regretfully. She

kissed him again but this time he did not let
her move away from him. His arms tightened
round her and Nanny, opening the door to
bring in tea, closed it softly, deciding that
toasted scones were not as important as love.

*　　　*　　　*

Kennedy linked his arm through Nancy's as
they walked home in the soft evening light
towards the ranch cabin lent to them by
friends for the period of his recuperation. The
woods were golden with autumn tints. A mist
of grey smoke hung in the air above the cabin.
Inside, a blazing fire and long cold drinks
would be waiting to welcome them, yet he
lingered just a little longer in the open, cold
though it was becoming, wishing to savour the
happiness of the moment.

This week was like a dream come true—the
dream he had thought when he was in the
desert could never materialise. The ranch
house was the epitome of all he had planned
for his retirement and he and Nancy were
alone together, perfectly and totally alone.

'I feel a bit of a heel,' he told her
shamefacedly. 'We should have invited Bruce
and Eve to stay here with us. But I couldn't. I
wanted you all to myself—selfish brute that I
am.'

Nancy pressed his arm.

'Then if you are selfish, so am I. I'd have

188

hated it if you had invited them. Anyway, darling, how do you know they'd have wanted to come? From what Bruce told me in the hospital, I think he wanted to have Eve to himself every bit as much as we wanted to be by ourselves. I liked Eve, Max. I think she is just right for him.'

'No more match-making, then?' Kennedy asked his wife, gently teasing.

She smiled back at him.

'I have a feeling the die is cast. She'll make Bruce a good wife. I talked to her quite a bit, you know.'

'Does she love him?'

'I think so. Sounded like it to me.'

'And what does your woman's instinct tell you?'

He was teasing her again but with an underlying note of deep tenderness together with mysterious wonder. As long as he lived— and he intended to live every minute of the life that had been returned to him— Kennedy would never understand about Nancy's intuition; how, in the face of utter hopelessness, she had still hoped—more than hoped, firmly believed that he was safe.

'I just *knew* it, darling!' she had reiterated.

Would he have felt the same conviction about her safety had their positions been reversed? He'd asked himself this question a dozen times and did not know the answer. He imagined that he would have gone half out of his mind with worry and despair. He had always been ruled by logic and the logical facts were that the plane had disappeared for good. The world had accepted it—but not Nancy.

He himself had not believed at the end that rescue could come in time. He'd resigned himself to death, in so far as any human being desiring life can resign himself. That eleventh-hour reprieve had seemed a miracle . . .

'If I had died . . .' he said, more to himself than to his wife, 'do you think you would have known that, too?'

She nodded.

He thought about that little game of hers—the attempt she made to establish telepathic communication with him by uniting their thoughts at the identical moment of eleven p.m. In the past he'd played along to please her, but never believed. Now he wasn't so sure.

'When you thought of me whilst I was out there in the desert,' he said, 'did all those longings of mine reach you somehow?'

'Longings?' She looked at him with a puzzled frown. 'Well, no, darling, not if you mean I felt your thirst or exhaustion or anything like that. It's hard to explain.'

'Try!' he urged her.

'Well, there was one night—Julia was downstairs in the bar having a drink and I was upstairs in my room on my bed resting. I was thinking intensely of you. I suppose I ought to have been unhappy, but strangely I wasn't in the least. You seemed very near, almost as if you were in the room with me. I felt—I don't know, Max—happy. It was as if you were in one of those moods you get from time to time when you start thanking me for everything and telling me what a good wife I've been and how much you love me—you know, darling. You get that way on occasions. In the early days of our marriage those moods made me wonder if you'd been unfaithful to me and that your expressing your love and gratitude was your way of showing remorse and making up for it. Then as the years went by, I came to accept those moments and treasure them for what they really were—you standing back, apart, looking in on our marriage and seeing it from the outside and being grateful. Does that sound crazy?'

'No, not at all. And that's exactly the way it was, out there in the Sahara. I was seeing you, our marriage, from a million miles away, nearly from another world. And I sat down and wrote to you, darling, telling you how grateful I was for everything. I don't know what happened to the letter. I looked for it one day at the hospital but I couldn't find it. Those Bedouins pinched practically everything any of us had—cigarette cases, clothes, the lot, Not that I hold it against them—they were welcome. But I wish now I still had that letter. It would have been interesting for you to see— work out if my thoughts really were reaching you.'

'But they must have been!' Nancy replied, not seeming in the least surprised. 'How else could I have been so certain you were alive?'

He laughed—suddenly loving her more than ever for her simple faith. Thank God he hadn't been taken from her. She loved and needed him just as she always had; just as he loved and needed her. This whole week had been like a glorious honeymoon for them—better by far, as Nancy said, than their real honeymoon. It would have to end, of course. There was the China crisis developing which would most surely embroil him. He hadn't told her about it because he did not want anything to spoil the perfection of this life up in the hills. A few more days was the most he could hope for—then back to Washington. But he wouldn't tell her till the time came.

They had reached the cabin. Nancy paused, standing on tiptoe to reach up and plant a quick kiss on his face.

'We'll be going home soon, won't we, Max? Time goes so quickly! I'll hate leaving but in a way I won't mind because we'll be going together.'

'Oh, Nance!' he whispered, hugging her to him. 'How did you guess?'

But she only smiled at him, kissed him again and drew him gently inside the door towards the comfort and the warmth.

The three girls sat in Janet's home, round the loaded tea table. Ann and Denise were teasing her mother about the quantity of food she had provided for them.

'It's been the same ever since I got back!' Janet admitted, looking at her mother fondly. 'She seems to think it was hunger I nearly died of and at every meal there's enough for at least six people!'

'Well, dear, you are looking the better for it nevertheless!' said Mrs Ross placidly.

The three girls had all lost a considerable amount of weight during their ordeal. Denise, always a plump girl, was determined to keep her new figure but Ann, tall and slender, seemed able to eat all she wanted and never add an ounce to the scales.

They laughed, happy to be together in such safe, homely surroundings. It was the first time they had sat down to a meal together since they'd left the Tripoli hospital individually with their parents. It was inevitable, therefore, that the meal over, they would begin to discuss their adventure.

Janet proudly displayed her new engagement ring. Allan had been a different person since she'd come home. It was as if the nature of their separation had given each of them an entirely new slant on each other. They were no longer childhood friends who had drifted into becoming sweethearts. Allan was fiercely possessive and demanding and the very real affection Janet had always had for him blossomed into love. They were to be married next spring.

The girls were teasing her now about her flirtation on board the V.C.10 with the radio operator. Had she told Allan about him? they asked her. Was he jealous? What would Janet pay them to keep quiet about her flirtation with him!

Denise, too, was on the point of engagement. She'd met and fallen head-over-heels in love with a young Scottish newspaper reporter who'd been in Tripoli to cover the story of their rescue. They were to become engaged, she told her friends, as soon as he'd taken her home to Edinburgh to meet his family.

Only Ann remained heart free but did not seem in the least perturbed about it.

'One of the three of us needs to have their feet on the ground if we're to go ahead with our hairdressing establishment!' she said practically. 'Don't you agree, Mr Ross?'

Stories had appeared in the local paper about all three girls and their adventure and it was well known that they were going to start up a salon as soon as they had recuperated from their ordeal. The publicity would stand them in good stead.

The future seemed bright and rosy; the past

far away now in the familiar surroundings of home. Yet it was far from totally forgotten. All three admitted to waking with terrible nightmares. It was only to be expected, said Janet's Mum, that they'd all suffer a bit from shock for a while. What they needed, she told them, was a good long holiday right away somewhere.

The three girls burst out laughing. No one in this world, not the Queen herself, would talk them into moving one inch away from good old England. No more foreign holidays, thank you very much and most certainly no more flying.

'As far as I'm concerned,' said Janet, 'I don't mind if there are no more Pools wins, either. I can't say all that money bought any of us good luck. We could have died!'

For a moment there was silence as everyone thought how near death had been. For a brief second, fear so recently banished from them, filled the room. It slowly receded as Dad switched on the telly. Children's Hour gave way to the news. They listened with half an ear to the latest political developments and then to pictures of race rioting in the States. Suddenly, Janet grasped Denise's arm.

'Ssssh, all of you!' she commanded. 'Just look at that!'

For, a moment they all sat stunned by the clips of Larry Bell, snatches of film taken of him at some of his more important appearances. They were followed by pictures of Sarah on the arm of her father, Lord Finnon-Waters.

'Just fancy that—they're engaged!' said Janet's Mum, as always delighted by news of a forthcoming marriage. 'Do you think they'll invite you girls to the wedding? Fancy you going to a posh wedding like that!'

Janet laughed.

'Who said it would be a posh wedding, Mum, even if we are invited? Sarah wasn't a bit snobbish, was she, girls? You'd never have guessed she was an Honourable.'

The news was switched off and Sarah's and Larry's elopement, pseudonyms and false identities were discussed in detail with Mrs Ross 'fancy that-ing' and Dad saying 'whatever next!' It was good to laugh about any part of their terrible ordeal. They felt the better for it and decided to send a joint telegram congratulating the young couple on their engagement.

'Wonder what's happened to the others!' Janet mused. 'I wish there hadn't had to be any of us . . . dead.'

'That poor Mrs Carson and the sad little nanny,' said Denise thoughtfully.

'Or those sweet old-age pensioners. Seems awful they never got to see their daughter again after all those years.'

'Well, they'd had a good long life together,' Mrs Ross said cheerfully, determined not to let

196

the mood change to one of melancholy. 'Maybe it's all for the best. I'm sorry for the daughter, though, having her hopes raised like that at the end and then hearing her parents were dead. Still, she has those nice young children to console her. Ever so pretty they looked in the newspapers!'

'The pair I felt most sorry for was poor Mr and Mrs James!' said Ann.

Mrs Ross stared thoughtfully into the fire. As a mother, her sympathies went naturally to the parents of the dead girl, Jennifer, and yet she couldn't help feeling that maybe it was better the girl had died. Denise had told her that she was a drug addict and who could tell?—even if she had reached the hospital in South Africa, she might never have been cured. That was one death which might have been a merciful one in the circumstances.

'Well, at least they have something to live for now,' Ann was saying. 'I had a letter from Mrs James last week, telling me they plan to adopt two Vietnamese orphan babies. Don't you think that's fabulous?'

'And I had a letter, too, I wanted to tell you about,' said Denise. 'Mine was from Mary-Lou. She and John Wilson are getting married in Cornwall next month. She wanted us all to go to the wedding, but I suppose it's a bit far to go, really. Still, we can send her a present and a greetings wire.'

For a few moments they pondered happily

the choice of a suitable wedding gift, then Janet's father broke in with his more masculine train of thought.

'Wonder what those lads in the football team are up to!' he mused. 'Be a while before they're back in training. What a funny, mixed-up lot you were!'

'Well, that's life!' said Mrs Ross. 'Now what about my programme, Father? I don't like to miss my film, you know.'

The set was switched on and warmed up in time for the announcer to give out the title.

'*Sands of Time*!' he said. 'With Dirk . . .' Laughter drowned his voice.

'I'm not watching sands of anything,' laughed Janet. 'I've seen enough sand to last me the whole of my life.'

'Reckon you have, too,' said Dad tenderly and switched over to ITV.

*   *   *

Chris and Liz Barlow washed up the supper dishes in their tiny kitchen. He wore an apron, she black slacks.

They were laughing about it.

'Easy to see who wears the pants in this house!' he said, kissing the nape of her neck as she bent over the sink.

She gave a deep sigh of contentment.

'I suppose in a minute you'll be complaining about drying dishes on your honeymoon!'

'Not me!' Chris said. 'I think it was exactly the right thing to do, darling—coming home to our own flat. I'm beginning to *feel* married now and that's the way I like it. No more exotic honeymoons for me, thank you.'

'I don't ever want to think about it again!' Liz said, emptying the red plastic bowl and carefully wiping the stainless steel sink until it shone back at her. Oh, it was wonderful to be here alone with Chris, all their own belongings in their own little home and just the two of them! No more reporters or crowds of people pointing them out. She'd hated it, though as Chris pointed out, they should be grateful to the magazine which had paid them a large sum of money for their story of their ordeal. Without that cheque they wouldn't own all this furniture or the blue carpet in the sitting-room or the bedroom curtains.

In a month's time the article would be appearing in print—'A Different Kind of Honeymoon' the editor was going to call it. Well, different it certainly was from most people's honeymoons, being hi-jacked and nearly dying in the Sahara Desert and then living with a lot of Bedouins in tents.

Funny people, Chris mused. Kind, though, and they had saved their lives. But for them he and Liz wouldn't be here now, clearing away the supper and living like any normal couple. One day, perhaps, they'd go back out there and see if they could locate the tribe—thank them properly. If Liz wanted to. She was still very shaky after the ordeal and only really felt safe when he was around. He rather enjoyed her dependence on him, though fought against this because he wanted her to make as complete a recovery as he had. But there was lots of time. They both had sick leave from work and they still had another whole week alone together in the flat. Life was good. They'd been lucky. He was very, very happy.

He took off his apron, put away the tea towel and encircled Liz with two strong arms. She leant against him, sighing deeply.

'Happy?' he asked.

She turned and smiled up at him with radiant eyes.

CHAPTER TWELVE

The hotel in Paris was small, select, with wonderful food and terrible plumbing. They had a large brass bed with a huge feather coverlet which invariably slid off in the night. The French proprietress, with that wonderful instinct for love, saw that they were completely undisturbed.

Eve laughed as the sound of footsteps receded down the stairs. Since they had not called *'Entrez!'* that first morning when the *femme de chambre* knocked, they knew from past experience that breakfast would have been left discreetly outside the bedroom door.

Bruce yawned, climbed out of bed, pushed open the shutters and drew in a deep breath of air. Then, shuddering with the cold, closed the windows and pattered across the room in bare feet to collect the breakfast tray and take it back to bed. The smell of good French coffee and warm rolls was irresistible.

'I'm sure Madame thinks we are lovers!' Eve said, as she poured out coffee. 'Are we going to disillusion her, darling, and tell her we are really and truly married?'

Bruce bit into a crisp roll and shook his head.

'No! Her look of delight when you signed your maiden name instead of Mallory was too good to spoil.'

They both laughed, remembering Eve's absent-minded signature in the register when they'd arrived tired after their wedding ceremony. It hadn't been easy getting a special licence and completing all the formalities necessary for a sudden marriage in a foreign country. But Bruce had brooked no delays.

'If I give you time to think you might change your mind!' he'd told Eve, only half jokingly. 'I don't intend to risk it.'

He'd asked her three times to marry him whilst they were recuperating in the Tripoli hospital. Eve had been tempted to say yes right away but she was afraid of her own feelings. They'd been through so much and were still in such poor physical condition that she was afraid they—Bruce in particular—might be proposing marriage on a kind of reaction. She told him she wanted time to think about it but Bruce had persisted with such determination and conviction that in the end she had agreed.

Now, she could laugh at her hesitation. In retrospect it was impossible for her to understand how she could have doubted the 'rightness' of their marriage. They were perfectly, wonderfully and ideally suited. And Bruce was a wonderful lover—tender, thoughtful, kind and intensely adoring. She'd never imagined she could be so happy.

They were exploring Paris, their days filled with laughter and good food and wine. They were discovering each other. The past, for both of them, had lost its nostalgia and was erased by the new memories they were creating. Though new and young and exciting, theirs was a mature love and expanding with each day and night they shared.

At the end of their second week they would be leaving Paris to fly to Washington. Bruce would be needed by Kennedy Maxwell to prepare for the China talks. He tried not to think about work, for inevitably he would have to leave Eve for weeks at a time just as Maxwell had had so often to leave Nancy. Sometimes, of course, wives could go with their husbands but not always, and he was not sure if he could bear to be parted from Eve.

'Darling, of course we'll bear it!' Eve said practically. 'You know you love your work really. Nancy was telling me in Tripoli how you and Maxwell become so totally immersed in it that you even forget to eat! Besides, think how wonderful it will be when you come home— each time like a honeymoon all over again.'

'Except that it won't be in Paris,' Bruce sighed. 'One day, when I retire, I'd like to live here. I think I'm a European at heart—no doubt my Swedish ancestry coming to the fore. How about you, darling? No hankering to live in England?'

She shook her head.

'I've nothing to keep me in England,' she said. 'I shan't mind where I live, Bruce, so long as it is with you—Washington, Paris, China, if you like—just so long as we're together!'

'What about our kids? They'll have to go to school.'

'I won't want children if having them means we'd be separated!" Eve replied. But already they had talked about the family they wanted —not large; if possible one of each. Her longing one day to have children surprised Eve. She had never thought much about it. But now she knew that she wanted Bruce's children. She wanted them for herself and for him, because he loved kids. She knew from Nancy how popular he was with children and could imagine him as a perfect father. Whether she would be a perfect mother was more questionable. For her, the man she loved would come first. Perhaps that was a good thing. Children grew up, left home. In Tripoli she'd listened to Nancy's description of her own life with Kennedy and envied her the wonderful relationship she had with her husband. Now she was beginning to understand how such a relationship could grow over the years. In one week her love for Bruce had intensified beyond all belief. His constant care of her and love for her evoked a continual growing response within her. He seemed to feel the same way.

'I'm lucky!' she thought. 'We didn't really know each other very well. We might not have liked each other!' There were a hundred little ways in which they might not have suited each other. Yet it had all proved perfect—too perfect to believe in completely. The time must come when they disagreed, quarrelled even, felt out of tune. But basically she was beginning to feel secure because they really liked each other. It wasn't turning out, as she'd half feared, to be nothing more than infatuation or desire.

Sometimes, though not so often now, she thought about the plane trip which had brought them together. The horror of those last two days before rescue could still start her shivering . . . the stench of the bodies in the hot sun when none of them had the strength to bury the dead; the torturing thirst; the heat; the slow acceptance and finally longing for death. The ensuing days when she was being cared for by the Bedouins were hazy. Mostly she remembered the taste in her mouth of that warm goat's milk; the brown eyes and skin of the Bedouin woman who bathed her with rank oil; the intense relief of waking to find Bruce sitting nearby watching her from eyes set in a gaunt, blistered, unshaven face, and of knowing that he and she were alive.

There were times when she felt the whole adventure was just a nightmare, unreal, imagined. Bruce had confessed that he, too, was beginning to doubt they'd ever lived through such happenings.

It was better, they decided, not to try to remember. Too many had died. They had, themselves, come too close to death. Perhaps, when more time had elapsed, they would talk about it with greater equanimity, less emotion. Time healed everything in due course. None knew it better than Bruce who had once believed himself beyond consolation after his wife's death in childbirth. If he had had to come very close to death himself in order to realise that he was in love again, with Eve, then he was glad it had all happened the way it had. He might, despite his assurances to her to the contrary, have never seen her again if that plane had landed on schedule and he and

Kennedy had become caught up in the Cairo crisis. Busy as they always were on such missions, Eve's memory might have taken on a different guise; become just an attractive girl who would have been fun to know better. He might never have gone in search of her; their paths never have crossed again.

The thought was unbearable. He put the breakfast tray back on the landing and locked the door. A moment later, he was holding her tightly in his arms.

'Oh, darling!' she whispered. 'I'm not going to run away.'

His grasp on her eased a little and he let out a long sigh.

'No, I know,' he said. 'I just felt suddenly how incredibly important you are to my happiness. I couldn't bear it if this—not the other—was a dream and I woke up and found I'd just dreamed you! I love you, Eve, I love you!'

This time it was she who tightened her arms about him.

'I'm real enough,' she said tenderly. 'And I love you, too!'

And set about proving it.

*　　　*　　　*

Three months later the evening papers announced the news of another hi-jacking.
BOEING FORCED TO LAND IN CUBA,

screamed the headlines.

The home-going commuters discussed the incident. 'There was another one a short while ago, wasn't there?' asked one.

'Wasn't American, was it? Came down in the Gobi Desert, I seem to recall.'

'Wasn't that one last year?'

'I can't remember.'

The fate of the V.C.10 was nothing more than a forgotten item of yesterday's news.

EPILOGUE

Mrs Barlow senior was enjoying a cup of tea when her grand-daughter burst into the kitchen on her way back from school.

'I'm so glad you've dropped in, dear!' she said. 'I've some news for you—good news! Your mother and father have agreed to let you go on holiday with your friend, Lucy. I was able to convince them that the chances of anything awful happening to you on the journey were statistically so remote that . . .'

'Oh, Gran, I'm sorry!' the girl interrupted. 'Please don't think I'm not grateful for what you've been trying to do—'cos I am. But everything's changed now. I should have told you sooner. Cynthia has asked me to go pony trekking with her in Wales, and you know that riding's my most favourite of absolutely everything. Lucy's taking Gemma to Egypt, so it's all worked out perfectly, provided Mum and Dad say I can go to Wales . . .'

'I'm sure they will, dear. No one's likely to hi-jack a string of Welsh ponies, are they?!'

'I still think Mum and Dad were silly to worry . . . just because of something that happened ages and ages ago!'

'I know, dear!' said her grandmother. But secretly, she, too, was relieved.